MW00527117

Ada[illegible] From Laura's, Sighing Deeply.

"You are a fatally attractive woman," he murmured. "I understand better now...."

"Understand what?"

"How you managed to conquer all those men. If circumstances were different, I might be tempted to add myself to the list."

Tempted to add myself...

Laura blinked, like someone who had been rudely slapped awake. The aura of romance shattered, as if someone had just shot out the moon. Merciful heavens, what was she doing, kissing Adam Barnhardt, her sister's avowed enemy?

And not just kissing him, but *kissing* him, in the hot, intimate way of two lovers just before they—

Horrified, she thrust him away from her. "No, Mr. Barnhardt," she said in a choked voice. "You *don't* understand. That's exactly the trouble with you. You don't understand anything at all...."

Dear Reader,

You can tell from the presence of some *very* handsome hunks on the covers that something special is going on for Valentine's Day here at Silhouette Desire! That "something" is a group of guys we call "Bachelor Boys" . . . you know, those men who think they'll never get "caught" by a woman—until they do! They're our very special Valentine's Day gift to you.

The lineup is pretty spectacular: a *Man of the Month* by Ann Major, and five other fabulous books by Raye Morgan, Peggy Moreland, Karen Leabo, Audra Adams and a *brand-new* to Silhouette author, Susan Carroll. You won't be able to pick up just one! So, you'll have to buy all six of these delectable, sexy stories.

Next month, we have even more fun in store: a *Man of the Month* from the sizzling pen of Jackie Merritt, a delicious story by Joan Johnston, and four more wonderful Desire love stories.

So read . . . and enjoy . . . as these single guys end up *happily* tamed by the women of their dreams.

Until next month,

Lucia Macro
Senior Editor

Please address questions and book requests to:
Reader Service
U.S.: P.O. Box 1325, Buffalo, NY 14269
Canadian: P.O. Box 1050, Niagara Falls, Ont. L2E 7G7

SUSAN CARROLL

BLACK LACE AND LINEN

SILHOUETTE Desire®
TM
Published by Silhouette Books
America's Publisher of Contemporary Romance

If you purchased this book without a cover you should be aware that this book is stolen property. It was reported as "unsold and destroyed" to the publisher, and neither the author nor the publisher has received any payment for this "stripped book."

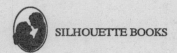

SILHOUETTE BOOKS

ISBN 0-373-05840-3

BLACK LACE AND LINEN

Copyright © 1994 by Susan Coppula

All rights reserved. Except for use in any review, the reproduction or utilization of this work in whole or in part in any form by any electronic, mechanical or other means, now known or hereafter invented, including xerography, photocopying and recording, or in any information storage or retrieval system, is forbidden without the written permission of the editorial office, Silhouette Books, 300 East 42nd Street, New York, NY 10017 U.S.A.

All characters in this book have no existence outside the imagination of the author and have no relation whatsoever to anyone bearing the same name or names. They are not even distantly inspired by any individual known or unknown to the author, and all incidents are pure invention.

This edition published by arrangement with Harlequin Enterprises B. V.

® and TM are trademarks of Harlequin Enterprises B. V., used under license. Trademarks indicated with ® are registered in the United States Patent and Trademark Office, the Canadian Trade Marks Office and in other countries.

Printed in U.S.A.

SUSAN CARROLL

began her career by writing Regency romances. It was a long way from the starch of the British aristocracy to the sizzle of a contemporary American love story. But, in making the leap, Susan found one thing remained the same: that spark of humor that gives zest to any romance, no matter what the time period.

Susan draws on the same humor in her own life. Currently residing in Illinois, she keeps busy between books, coping with her two lively children, two rambunctious cats and one very noisy hamster.

To my agent, Eileen Fallon, for all her enthusiasm and encouragement.

One

The man was staring at her.

Laura Stuart felt certain of that, even though she could make out little more than the shadow of his six-foot-something frame at the other end of the hotel parking garage. As she bent to unlock the trunk of the rental compact, she cast an uneasy glance over her shoulder.

She found herself thinking of every movie she had ever seen where some lone victim was shot, stabbed, blown up or otherwise made miserable in the deserted cavern of a parking garage.

"Don't get paranoid, Laura," she murmured, attempting to put the brakes on her rampant imagination. The man lingering in the next aisle was probably only a parking attendant or one of the hotel guests who couldn't remember where he'd parked his car. Her nerves were getting the better of her because she was tired and hot. It had taken her nearly five hours to drive from Bennington Falls. The shorebound traffic to Ocean City shouldn't have been so bad on a Thursday night, but she had gotten lost several times and an accident on the parkway had snarled up things for miles. The air-conditioning in the car she'd rented had given out long before she'd exited the New Jersey turnpike.

Her once-crisp linen suit was damp and sticky. Her shoulder-length dark brown hair was a windblown tangle. Her nylons felt fused to the bottom of her feet and—

And that man was making her very nervous.

She heard the hollow echo of his footsteps and realized that he had shifted position. Out of the corner of her eye, she noted that he now lurked by the broad concrete pillar with the sign proclaiming this section of the garage to be Level Two. Laura had no better impression of him than before, except that he was very tall and broad shouldered.

She pulled one small satchel out of the trunk and decided that the rest of her luggage could wait until she checked into the hotel. Better yet, it could wait until morning when this place would be bustling with arriving and departing guests.

Steeling her shoulders, she started forward, her heels clicking against the concrete in a staccato rhythm. She tried to remember everything she had learned from the self-help book she had recently purchased, filled with advice for women who travel alone.

Walk briskly and with confidence. Don't look like a victim. Stay alert. Whistle a happy tune.

No, that was from the *King and I* or was it—Laura's nervous thoughts broke off abruptly. She gave a small gasp as the man stepped away from the pillar. Only a few yards separated them. She could see him more clearly now, the glow from the yellow light overhead illuminating his features.

He was wearing a formal white dinner jacket and a black tie, but somehow that did not make him look any less menacing. He blocked her path to the elevator, his hands placed on his hips in a challenging stance.

"L.C.?" he said.

The query made no sense. As he stalked closer, Laura had a strange sensation of being overpowered, and yet he made no threatening gesture. She gained a fleeting impression of hard, chiseled features set in a tanned face, a faint scar creasing a granite jaw. Sun-streaked ash blond hair waved back from a high, broad brow. But it was the storm of his wintry gray eyes that arrested her attention and caused her heart to hammer.

"I beg your pardon?" she stammered.

Don't speak to strangers. That was not the book's warning, but her grandmother's.

"I've been waiting for the chance to be alone with you," he said.

His deep voice rumbled in her ears like distant thunder.

"No, thank you," she said, slipping past him and rushing toward the elevator. "I'm not interested."

She grimaced. Her parents had done too good a job of instilling manners in her. It was not necessary to be polite to aggressive men who accosted you in parking garages.

She jabbed at the elevator button. Her heart sank to her toes when she heard him following.

"Look, I just want to talk," he said in a tone of rising impatience.

"Stay away from me!"

She cried out in relief when the elevator doors slid open. But before she could dart inside, the man's hand clamped about her wrist. The unexpected contact startled her. As she struggled to free herself, the car keys dropped from her fingers.

"I don't give up that easily, Miss Stuart," he said, tightening his grip.

His touch alarmed Laura far more than his angry words; the heat of his palm against her wrist, the strength she sensed in those long, tanned fingers.

Don't be afraid to scream, the book had advised.

Laura drew breath, but her throat seemed to have shut. Forget the book! She acted on pure instinct. Swinging her satchel, she levered a blow at the man's head, catching him right between the eyes.

With a startled grunt, he released her. Laura dove into the elevator just as the doors began to close. Desperately, she punched at the lobby button, any button.

The doors slid shut the instant her attacker regained his balance. She had one last glimpse of his face. He actually had the nerve to look stunned.

As the elevator hummed into movement, Laura leaned back against one of its support railings. Like most hotel elevators, this one was incredibly slow, but she was safe. Safe. She drew in a deep breath and attempted to slow her racing pulse. At one time such an experience would have been enough to set off one of her asthma attacks. Thank God, she had finally grown past that, although she still carried an inhaler just in case. She groped inside her satchel until she found the smooth metal-and-plastic device, fingering it like a talisman until her heart resumed a more steady rhythm.

Her car keys were still lying down there on the garage floor, but she wasn't going back for them, not unless accompanied by a burly security guard—perhaps two. A fine beginning to her vacation, she thought glumly. Before she'd even checked in, she was going to have to find the hotel detective and report that she had been menaced by—by—

A well-dressed stranger who had murmured sinister suggestions and called her by name. Laura stiffened as that realization hit her.

He knew her name. He had called her Miss Stuart. She wasn't sure if that made her feel better or worse. Could it possibly be she had met him before? No, she would never have forgotten a face like his, with those storm-cloud eyes.

What then? Had he recognized her, perhaps from the bio on the back of one of her books, and decided to pursue her? A deranged fan? An angry parent? She wrote books for young children, for heaven's sake, whimsical tales of mischievous woodland creatures. Nothing controversial enough to get her stalked by a rugged stranger in a white dinner jacket.

Of course, there was one other possibility. Laura frowned. A case of mistaken identity. She was still considering that one when the elevator doors shuddered open.

The lobby of the Sea King Hotel was practically deserted. The glass doors that led to the restaurant and the gift shop were both locked, the windows glazed dark.

Even the clerk had stepped away from the reception desk. The only signs of life emanated from the open doors of the banquet room, the blare of a voice distorted through a microphone, the faint smattering of applause.

Laura headed in that direction, hoping to snare one of the waiters milling about and ask where she could find the security guard. As she paused on the threshold, attempting to adjust her eyes to the ballroom's softer mood lighting, she received her second jolt of the evening.

Over the speaker system, someone announced, "And now for our final guest, I am privileged to present to you, that award-wining children's author, Miss L.C. Stuart."

Laura froze at the outburst of applause that swelled from the sea of linen-covered tables. All thoughts of security guards, parking garages and threatening strangers were driven out of her head. Her hand fluttered self-consciously toward her throat.

It took her a stunned moment to realize that no heads were swiveling in her direction. All eyes remained riveted upon the podium at the front of the room. Laura was tempted to pinch herself. She had to have strayed into the midst of some bizarre dream.

A dream that grew stranger by the minute as she observed *herself* weaving between the tables to step into the spotlight by the microphone. At least the young woman was a very plausible imitation of Laura Caroline Stuart. Her slender figure was enhanced by a romantic, flowing silk dress with a high Victorian-style collar and puffed sleeves. She had the same heart-shaped face as Laura, the same finely arched brows, the same slim, straight nose. Her dark brown hair, a close approximation of Laura's own shade, was swept up into a prim chignon. Wire-rimmed glasses framed eyes that Laura knew were hazel, just as her own.

But I don't wear glasses, Laura thought irrelevantly.

As her initial shock wore off, Laura muttered, "Chelsey Stuart! *Now* what in heaven's name are you up to?"

Inching farther into the room, Laura watched her twin sister's performance at the podium. She was vaguely aware that Chelsey was delivering a stirring speech about raising the level of literacy in America, one of Laura's favorite projects.

"It's never too soon to develop a love of reading in our children," Chelsey said. "Back when I started my first book, chronicling the adventures of Furballs Bunny—"

"That's *Fur Toes,*" Laura mumbled under her breath. As indignation at her sister's antics took over, Laura scarcely heard the rest of Chelsey's speech.

It was mercifully brief. After the final round of applause, Chelsey minced down from the platform. Laura was not sure what outraged her more, the fact that her sister was impersonating her or the way Chelsey was doing it. Like some fussy maiden librarian.

The room's lights came up. Chelsey was swallowed from sight by a throng of people pressing forward to congratulate her and shake her hand. Laura remained at the back of the room, still gripping her satchel. She bided her time, thinking of all the things she meant to say to Chelsey as soon as she got her alone, all of them quite pithy and to the point.

But beneath her anger, Laura felt sick at heart. It was not supposed to be this way. When she had managed to finish her latest book early, she had been seized by a rare impulse. She knew Chelsey had been spending her summer in Ocean City, booked in at the Sea King Hotel. Working on a photographic essay, Chelsey had said.

Laura had hoped to drive down from Bennington Falls and surprise Chelsey. A surprise meant to give her and Chelsey time alone together, to heal some of the wounds left from their previous meeting.

Echoes of the quarrel she and Chelsey had had six months ago in Bennington Falls still played through Laura's mind....

"When will you ever stop trying to act like my mother, Laura? Our own mother has never wanted the job, and that's fine with me. What makes you think you have to fill in for her?"

"Because I love you, Chelsey. When I saw your picture splashed all over the tabloids with that Xavier Storm, I couldn't help being concerned about you. As your older sister—"

"Older! By two minutes. Two lousy minutes."

"You manage to make me feel two decades older."

"Maybe if you weren't buried alive here in this rinky-dink town with your damned books, maybe if you ever had some male company beside Furballs Bunny, you wouldn't have so much time to worry about who *I'm* dating. Get a life, Laura."

Of course, Chelsey was apt to say anything when she was angry, things she did not mean. Laura had wanted to argue that she did have a life. It surrounded her in the fortress of her high-security apartment, in the countless awards for her writing displayed in her den, in her sketching table set up by the patio window, in the testimonials from the grateful citizens of Bennington Falls for her work in various charitable causes, in the ring tucked away in the drawer from her broken engagement. . . .

But Chelsey's bitter words had had just enough truth in them to sting. Laura and Chelsey had patched things up on the phone since then, and on the surface their relationship had returned to normal. But even across the miles of telephone wire, Laura could sense the tension humming between them.

Laura had hoped this visit would ease some of that tension. Given Chelsey's current escapade, that did not seem likely.

As the other guests filed past her, Laura positioned herself in front of the door where Chelsey would have to see her. When Chelsey finally glanced her way and their eyes met, Chelsey's mouth fell open.

She drew in a deep breath and cried out, "My God! What are you doing here?"

"I'm glad to see you, too," Laura said dryly.

Chelsey rushed forward and flung her arms about Laura in a swift hug. "Of course I'm glad to see you. But why didn't you tell me you were coming? I'm so surprised."

"Not half as much as I am."

Chelsey moistened her lips and lowered her voice to a whisper, "I know what you must be thinking, Laura. Just give me a chance. I can explain everything, but not here."

Before Laura could protest, Chelsey seized her by the arm and propelled her from the banquet room, all the while continuing to look furtively from side to side. The next thing Laura knew, she was being thrust into the pink opulence of a ladies' room.

For a brief moment she and Chelsey were reflected side by side in a gilt-trimmed mirror. It was strange and a little sad,

Laura thought. During their childhood, Laura's bouts of illness had frequently made her look paler and thinner than Chelsey. Then came adolescence and Chelsey's bouts of rebellion, doing everything from bleaching her hair to whacking it off and spiking it.

But never had the physical resemblance between them been closer, and never had she and Chelsey seemed further apart than at this moment. Except for the fact that Chelsey was a little more tan and had those ridiculous wire-rims slipping down her nose, the face in the mirror was identical to Laura's own.

"So when did you start wearing glasses?" Laura asked.

"Since they had a sale at the five-and-dime." Chelsey grinned and whipped off the wire-rims. "Only $13.95."

"They'll ruin your eyes."

"Mom used to tell me the same thing about having sex. But I'm still twenty-twenty." Chelsey laughed.

Laura perched her satchel on the edge of the sink. Folding her arms across her chest, she maintained a stony front. Chelsey's own smile faded. She leaned up against the restroom door, effectively barring the way in or out.

"You're really upset with me this time, aren't you, Laura?" she asked.

"Upset with you?" Laura said, trying to keep her voice level. "Why would I be upset? I only traveled two hundred miles in the heat and traffic to spend some time with my sister, and then found myself entering the twilight zone. I had the daylights scared out of me in the parking garage by some strange man in a dinner jacket, who's probably a hit man for the mob and then—"

Laura paced off a few agitated steps in front of the row of glistening pink sinks. "And then I escape upstairs to find this banquet in progress and nearly have a heart attack when I hear myself being announced as the guest speaker. Only it isn't me, because you're me, and I'm no longer sure who

I'm supposed to be. And to top everything off, you're holding me prisoner in a pink bathroom."

"I'm sorry, Laura. Really, I have a reasonable explanation for all of this."

"I'm dying to hear it."

"The damnedest thing happened to me this summer." Chelsey rubbed the back of her neck, looking almost embarrassed. "I sort of fell in love with this man. His name is Luke Barnhart."

"Luke Barnhart? Whatever happened to that man who owned all those hotels, that Storm person?"

"There was never anything serious between Xavier and me. We had a few laughs together. But that's ancient history."

Ancient history? It had only been a few months ago. But Laura knew there was no use pointing that out to Chelsey. Her sister didn't measure time in quite the same way as the rest of the world.

"I think it's the real thing between Luke and me," Chelsey continued. "There's only one teeny problem. He thinks I'm you."

"And wherever do you suppose he got a foolish idea like that?"

"I don't know." Chelsey's face dimpled into a mischievous smile. "Perhaps because I've been pretending to be you this past month or two."

Laura's jaw dropped open in dismay. "You've been impersonating me all summer?"

"I couldn't help it. I was in a desperate jam after that little affair with Xavier Storm—and don't you dare say 'I told you so,' Laura."

Laura wasn't going to, but she supposed there was no law against thinking it.

"Things were getting messy with Xavier's divorce, and for some reason the press decided to label me as the 'other woman,' even though Xavier had been separated from his wife long before he ever met me." Chelsey blew out a sigh of frustration. "The reporters and photographers just wouldn't leave me alone, especially the ones from those sleazy tabloids. They hounded me every time I set foot out of the hotel. Short of burying myself alive out there on the beach, I didn't know what else to do until I got this great idea of pretending to be you. After all, no one would want to interview you for anything, unless it was the next issue of *Humpty Dumpty.*"

"Thank you so much," Laura said dryly.

"Oh, you know what I mean. Anyway, it worked like a charm. As you, I told the reporters that Chelsey Stuart was off on a long European vacation, and they left me alone after that. Things didn't get complicated until this young man came up and asked me to autograph one of those books about Furballs for his little cousin."

"You've even been autographing my books?" Laura cried.

"I always could forge your signature. Hell, I can sign your name better than you can." Chelsey's sassy grin faded as she concluded, "That man was Luke Barnhart. He asked me to lunch, and before I knew it one thing led to another and then . . ."

"So all of this nonsense is because you've found a new boyfriend?"

"No. It's different this time, Laura, I swear it. I—I think I've fallen in love with Luke." Chelsey's voice faltered. "You don't believe me, do you?" She looked hurt. "Well, I guess I can't blame you for that. But, Laura, with all the men you've seen me go through, you've never heard me mention the *'L'* word before."

No, that was true, Laura thought, trying to be fair.

"It's different with Luke. It really is," Chelsey persisted. "When you meet him, you'll see. He's not even that good-looking. But what he is, is sweet and shy and sensitive and he can play a saxophone to die for. And he's very smart, brilliant really and—"

Chelsey turned away, her voice going suddenly husky. "But the best thing about him is that he thinks I'm smart, too. He—he respects me, Laura. He thinks I'm something special."

Laura caught sight of something wet glistening on Chelsey's cheek and was stunned. She couldn't remember the last time she had seen Chelsey cry.

The last of her annoyance with her sister melting away, Laura went to Chelsey, pressing her hand. "You *are* something really special, Chelsey Stuart," she murmured.

Chelsey gave a too-careless kind of shrug. "At least you and Luke seem to think so. But as usual, I've made an awful mess of everything. What am I going to do, Laura?"

"Tell Luke the truth," Laura said gently, offering her sister a tissue.

"Humph!" Chelsey sniffed, dashing her eyes across the back of her sleeve instead. "I might've known you'd come up with an impractical suggestion like that."

"You have no choice, Chelsey. You can't keep this deception up forever. If Luke cares for you, he'll understand."

"*You* don't understand." Chelsey shook her head miserably. "It's not that easy. Luke comes from this wealthy family, and he has this Uncle Adam who acts as his trustee. The guy's a hard-nosed, stiff-necked pain in the— And he hardly likes me as L.C. Stuart. What would Adam Barnhart think if he knew I was really the infamous twin, the original bad seed?"

"You don't need to worry about what this Uncle Adam thinks," Laura chided.

"Yes, I do. Luke respects Adam's opinion beyond anybody's." Chelsey fretted her lower lip. "All I need is a little more time, Laura. For me and Luke to be more sure of our feelings, for Luke to get to know me better."

"How can he get to know you better when you're pretending to be someone else?"

"I'm just so scared, Laura. Luke's the best thing that ever happened to me. I don't want to lose him. You've got to help me."

"What is it you want me to do? Go away again? Go back to Bennington Falls?"

"No!" Chelsey clutched at her. "I'm glad you came. I could use some moral support. Maybe you could even do something with Adam Barnhart. You've always been good at handling crotchety uncles."

"I don't see how that would work. There can't be two Laura Stuarts running around."

"No-o-o-o," Chelsey said slowly. "But there could be a Laura and a Chelsey."

Laura felt her blood turn cold. "Oh, no. No way! There is no way I could possibly pretend to be you."

"Sure you could. If I dressed you up in some of my more daring clothes . . ."

"This whole thing is crazy enough without me making it any worse."

"It would only be for a little while. A day or two at the most. You were always such a Goody Two Shoes when we were kids. You never would agree to swap places when I wanted to, even for a joke. I figure you owe me one."

Laura felt she owed her sister a lot more than that. All the puppies and kittens that could never be brought home because of Laura's asthma, all the missed softball games, talent shows, swim meets that Chelsey had spent with Laura in the hospital, the twelfth birthday celebrated watching Laura in an oxygen tent.

But two grown women trading places? It was pure lunacy.

"As your older sister—" Laura began.

"By two minutes. Two crummy minutes."

"I ought to put a stop to this insanity right now."

"Please, Laura." Chelsey said, making her eyes go wide and pleading. That wistful, big-eyed look had made Laura set aside her better judgment upon more than one occasion.

"But as the sister who loves you..." Laura sighed. "Oh, I suppose you can start calling me Chelsey."

Chelsey beamed and caught Laura in an exuberant hug. "Good girl. I knew I could count on you. Come on. I'm dying to have you meet Luke. He was here with me at the banquet tonight, but after my speech he went to try to find his uncle. The only reason I accepted this literacy gig was because I hoped my talk would impress Adam Barnhart, but the old grouch never showed up."

As if she feared Laura might change her mind, Chelsey began tugging her toward the door. She drew up short, frowning as she eyed Laura up and down.

"Damn! We're going to have to do something about you. Look at those clothes!"

Laura smoothed the lapel of her linen jacket. "This happens to be a designer suit, Chelsey, from one of the most exclusive boutiques in Bennington Falls."

"Bennington Falls! The hub of the fashion world." Chelsey rolled her eyes. "Well, there's no time for you to change into anything of mine right now. But at least lose that awful jacket."

Ruthlessly, Chelsey stripped the linen garment down Laura's arms. Uttering a small moan of protest, Laura watched as Chelsey wadded up three hundred dollars worth of designer original and stuffed it in Laura's satchel. She swiftly undid several of the buttons on Laura's blouse. "There! Not perfect, but it'll have to do for now."

"Chelsey!" Laura glanced with dismay at her exposed décolletage.

But Chelsey smacked her fingers away when Laura attempted to repair the damage. "Don't worry about a thing. You look fine." Chelsey gave her another swift hug, her eyes shining. "Oh, Laura, thank you. You won't be sorry for helping me with this."

"I think I'm sorry already," Laura mumbled.

She only had time to grab her satchel before Chelsey hauled her back out of the bathroom.

The lobby was nearly as deserted as when Laura had first arrived at the hotel. But a few of the guests were wandering outside the open door of the banquet room, including a young man in a dark jacket and crooked tie who glanced about with a vague expression, looking lost.

"That's my Luke," Chelsey whispered in Laura's ear, pointing out the blond-haired man.

"Oh," was all Laura could say. He seemed so...so young. Luke Barnhart appeared the sort most mothers would have deemed "a nice boy," more intelligent looking than handsome.

As they crossed the lobby, Chelsey startled Laura by muttering, "Damn! It looks like good old Uncle Adam finally showed up."

Laura craned her neck, trying to see who Chelsey meant. There was a little gray-haired bulldog of a man standing off to Luke's left, but he moved away in the company of a buxom redhead. The only other male in sight had his back to Laura. Her gaze skimmed over a pair of broad shoulders in a white dinner jacket that was disturbingly familiar. Her heart slammed against her ribs.

"Chelsey..." she began, trying to hang back.

But Chelsey hauled her forward, calling out merrily, "Hi, guys. Look who turned up here tonight to surprise me."

Luke smiled at Laura, a shy smile that was a little lop-sided but reflected all the way to the depths of his velvet brown eyes. Yet she scarcely noticed him as the towering male at his side came slowly around.

It *was* her stranger from the garage.

Laura shrank back instinctively, holding her satchel in front of her like a shield. His cold gray eyes flicked from Laura to Chelsey and back again. The heavy line of his ash-colored brows drew together as he obviously realized the mistake he had made earlier, and his jaw tightened. He did not appear the sort of man who appreciated being made to feel like a fool.

Laura was vaguely aware of being introduced to Luke Barnhart, shaking his hand.

"I'm so glad to meet you at last, Chelsey," the young man said. "L.C. has told me so much about you."

"L.C.?" Laura repeated faintly, unable to tear her eyes away from the hard-visaged man at Luke's side.

"You know I've never been comfortable being called Laura," Chelsey said glibly. "All my friends here at the shore just call me by my initials."

All her friends and one who was definitely not Chelsey's friend. Laura's memory jolted back to the first thing that hostile stranger had ever said to her.

"L.C.?"

The daunting realization washed over Laura even before Chelsey thought to complete the introductions.

"Oh, no," Laura murmured in disbelief, staring deep into those storm-cloud eyes.

"Not—not *Uncle Adam.*"

Two

"Actually the name is Barnhart, Adam Barnhart," he corrected, his ice gray eyes never leaving Laura's face. He extended his hand. Laura was not sure she wanted to take it.

She was given no choice. He captured her hand in his strong grasp. She found his touch warm and disturbing, sending a shiver through her. He was not perhaps as tall or as muscle-bound as she had imagined him to be in the garage's dim light. But Adam Barnhart had a definite physical presence.

"So we meet again, Miss Stuart," he said.

"You two know each other?" Chelsey asked.

"Your sister and I already bumped into each other this evening, L.C." Adam touched the bridge of his nose, and Laura saw a faint bruise.

The heat crept into Laura's cheeks. She managed to get back her hand and stammered, "Of course, at our first meeting Mr. Barnhart didn't take the time to introduce himself."

She felt as if she were still reeling from the shock. The man she had clobbered in the garage was Adam Barnhart. Good, old Uncle Adam, the grouch, the crotchety relation Chelsey had described to Laura.

Laura wondered if her sister might not need glasses after all.

"You missed the whole banquet, Uncle Adam," Luke complained. "And L.C.'s speech. She was sensational."

"I had a bit of . . . car trouble."

Laura started when Adam Barnhart reached for her hand again. She felt him press something cold and metallic into her palm. Her car keys.

"I believe these belong to you," he said.

"Car keys?" Chelsey chortled. "You mean *you* actually drove down from Bennington Falls?"

"Certainly," Laura snapped, a little defensively. Just because she generally traveled no farther than the Bennington Falls library did not mean she was incapable of venturing further if she put her mind to it.

"Good for you, babe," Chelsey started to say, then caught herself in time. "Er, yes, that's right. I keep forgetting how independent you are, Chelsey." She draped her arm about Laura's shoulders. "You must be tired. You haven't even had a chance to check in yet. You'll share my room, of course."

Without waiting for an answer, Chelsey took Laura's satchel away from her. "Is this your only bag?"

"No, the rest are still in the trunk of my car."

"Give me the keys. Luke and I will fetch what's left. What kind of car were you driving?"

"It's a light blue hatchback. The license number is on the key ring, but I don't think—" Laura started to protest, but Chelsey had already seized the keys.

"Luke and I will take care of everything, hon. You just relax and get better acquainted with Adam."

Shaking her head in a firm negative, Laura tried to catch Chelsey's eyes. But when Chelsey made up her mind to do something, she moved like a sandstorm, whirling at gale force, leaving one blinking and unsure of one's bearings.

Before Laura knew where she was at, Chelsey and Luke had vanished into the elevator, Chelsey giving Laura an encouraging smile and a breezy little wave as the doors closed.

Blast you, Chelsey, Laura fumed.

As her sister disappeared from view, Laura was very much aware of Adam Barnhart's cool appraisal. His gaze made her conscious of her windblown hair and the fact that Chelsey had undone way too many of the buttons on Laura's blouse. The silken material gaped open just above the lacy dip of her bra. Trying to act casual, Laura fumbled with the lowest undone button on her blouse, managing to work the pearl stem back through the hole. Adam's eyes seemed to rivet on the movement of her fingers with almost unwilling fascination.

An awkward silence ensued and Laura thought this might be a good moment for mutual apologies, a chance to make a fresh start with Adam. She cleared her throat and summoned a gracious smile.

"I'm sorry for the misunderstanding earlier, Mr. Barnhart. I hope I didn't hurt you. I didn't want to hit you, but you frightened me."

"That wasn't my intention. I thought you were your sister."

Adam appeared to think this curt explanation took care of everything. Laura's smile faded. She should end this deception and set Mr. Barnhart straight right now. Trying to help her sister through this disaster, even attempting to charm some gray-haired old curmudgeon was one thing. But playing the part of Chelsey for this sexy-looking man, who appeared like someone who had stepped straight out of a spy novel, was more than Laura had bargained for.

Yet she had promised Chelsey, and betraying her without giving her the chance to explain to Luke first would be nothing short of cruel.

Sighing, Laura said, "I doubt my sister—er, L.C.—would have appreciated being manhandled in that fashion, either."

"I don't make a habit of grabbing women in parking garages—"

"I'm relieved to hear it."

"But your sister is very difficult to pin down. I need to have a serious talk with L.C., and she keeps avoiding me."

Laura could well understand his frustration. She almost started to say that there were times when she had wanted to take hold of her flighty sister and—

But Laura checked herself. That would be too much like sympathizing with the enemy. And Laura was beginning to get a definite sense that Adam Barnhart was an adversary to be reckoned with.

Instead, she replied, "I see. And may I ask what this matter is, that's so urgent?"

"You can ask," he drawled. "But I very much doubt you would understand."

"Try me," Laura said, frowning.

But before he could reply, they were both obliged to step aside for several waiters carting trays of empty glasses from the banquet room.

"We seem to be in the way here. Perhaps this discussion would be best continued outside by the pool." He jerked his head in the direction of a glass door. "There's a nice breeze coming in off the ocean. It would be cool and quiet there."

"Also dark and deserted."

For the first time, the hint of a smile softened Adam's hard features. "I promise you have nothing more to fear from me. You swing a mean suitcase."

"You were just lucky I was out of Mace."

"You use that much of it?" He arched one brow, looking as if he suspected her of being some hysterical female, leaving a trail of blinded men littering every garage she passed through.

"I mean I loaned my Mace to Chel—to a friend of mine and then she forgot to— Never mind. Let's go."

Let's go? What was she saying? The last thing Laura wanted was to find herself alone with Adam Barnhart. Perhaps she didn't have to fear him grabbing her again, but there was a disquieting edge to the man.

Laura had always placed men into categories, comfortable and the not so comfortable, the sort who made one's heart skip ticks like a crazed alarm clock. The trouble was that Adam fell into the latter category, and Laura was more accustomed to the former.

She preferred the company of the sweet, helpless sort of male who needed aid with everything from fixing his tie to salvaging his soul. Adam did not look as if he had ever needed a woman for anything.

Except for satisfying the most primal male urges.

When he slipped his hand beneath her elbow to guide her through the glass doors leading out to the pool, Laura moved surreptitiously to do up another button on her blouse.

As soon as they reached the terrace, she was quick to draw away from him. The area was as deserted as she had anticipated it would be. The pool lights reflected upward, casting dancing patterns on the candy-striped hotel awning and the deck chairs that had been folded and stacked to one side. Even the boardwalk beyond the pool railing was deserted, except for a late-night jogger who passed by, his sneakers setting up hollow, lonely echoes on the planking.

Beyond that, Laura could make out the dark, moving shadow that was the sea, pounding against the shore in frothy white breakers, with a rhythm that was at once soothing and melancholy. Adam leaned against the railing that surrounded the pool, staring off toward the ocean.

Laura reflected that it was unusual to see any man bother with such formal attire these days, but she had to admit Barnhart wore the white jacket well, with an air of comfortable self-assurance. It was strange, because unlike his suit, his looks were anything but suave, smooth.

Riffled by the sea breeze, his shagged length of dark gold hair curled crisply against his collar. He had a high forehead and a hawklike nose, a hard jawline with its pale creasing of a scar. His deeply tanned face reminded her curiously of those jagged outcroppings of rock that seemed immovable, impervious, forever defying the batterings of the sea.

As though feeling the weight of Laura's stare, Adam shifted to face her. Resting one lean hip against the rail, he favored her with an assessment of his own that was bold and lingering and made Laura feel as if her blood thundered too close to the surface of her skin.

"So you are the notorious Chelsey Stuart," he said slowly. "If you don't mind my saying so, you don't look anything like your photographs."

"Photographs?"

"In the magazines and the papers."

Which ones did he mean? Laura was afraid to ask. With Chelsey, the possibilities were endless. She blushed. Had Barnhart seen photo spreads of Chelsey the time she had won the crown of Miss Seacomber in that skimpy French bathing suit, or had he noticed the tabloids when Chelsey had dressed as Lady Godiva to protest the closing of that nudist colony?

Or had he been following the reports of Chelsey's notorious string of affairs—the rock star, the playboy congressman, or Chelsey's most recent infamy, being cited as the other woman in hotel entrepreneur Xavier Storm's million-dollar divorce proceedings.

Whichever it was, small wonder that Adam stared at Laura, his face alight with pure male speculation, a curious blend of heat and arrogance. Laura was accustomed to neither. From the time she had been nineteen, men had already been respectfully referring to her as "ma'am."

"I believe we came out here to discuss L.C.," Laura reminded him crisply, her fingers inching up to close the next button on her blouse. "Exactly what has my sister been doing to make you feel you have to ambush her in a parking garage?"

It took Adam a moment to drag his eyes away from her blouse buttons. "I think I better wait and take that up with her."

"I suppose it has something to do with your nephew, Luke."

"Yes." After a slight hesitation, Barnhart added, "I wanted to request that your sister stay away from him."

Request? Why did that word on Adam Barnhart's lips sound more like "demand."

Laura stirred uneasily. Chelsey had said Barnhart did not approve of her relationship with Luke, but Laura had not expected anything quite this blunt, this final. She could understand why Chelsey's reputation might make any stern uncle a little leery, but Adam thought that Chelsey was Laura. And no one had ever disapproved of Laura Stuart.

Laura was surprised to find herself feeling a little piqued.

"And just what do you find wrong with me—I mean, L.C.?" she asked.

Barnhart jingled the change in his pocket and scowled. "I have nothing against your sister," he said at last. "It's only that Luke is a pretty naive kid. I don't want to see him get hurt. It would be very easy for him to be taken advantage of."

"You talk as if you think my sister plans to—to *ravish* Luke."

It was one of those lovely old-fashioned words that slipped into Laura's conversation from time to time. Her use of it had the strange effect of drawing Adam's eyes back to her blouse. She felt an even stranger surge of warmth as she fumbled with another button.

"No, I'm not afraid Luke might be *ravished,*" Barnhart said wryly. "But the kid is clearly out of his depth with an older woman."

"An older— How ancient do you think my sister and I are?"

"I have no idea. But I know how old my nephew is. He just turned twenty-two last month."

Laura was momentarily shocked herself. Twenty-two? Luke was little better than a teenage boy. What could Chelsey be thinking of? But defending her twin was like a knee-jerk reaction to Laura, and Adam had definitely applied a hammer. She rallied, saying, "Isn't that a double standard? I'll bet you wouldn't think anything of the age difference if Luke was a girl and L.C. was the man. And—and— Oh, you know what I mean."

"Yes, I do and, yes, it would still bother me. We're talking more than an age difference here. There's an even bigger gap in experience and maturity."

The experience, Laura was willing to grant him. As to maturity, Laura would not have been surprised if Luke didn't have an edge on Chelsey. But she kept that disloyal thought to herself.

"Excuse me, Mr. Barnhart," she said. "But I don't see what right you have trying to interfere. Luke seems old enough to make his own choices. Or if he needs advice, he can get it from his father."

"My brother is dead." Adam's flat tone gave away more than any deep expression of grief ever could have.

"I'm sorry," Laura said in more gentle tones.

Something flared in his eyes for a moment, something aching and vulnerable. He was quick to shutter it away again.

"I've acted as trustee for Luke and his younger sister ever since—" Adam paused, one hand reached up in a seemingly unconscious gesture to trace his scar. "Ever since—well, for a very long time. Not always an easy task."

"I'm sure it hasn't been."

"Especially since Luke inherited a sizable bit of money. Many women find that irresistibly attractive."

Laura understood what he was hinting at and she didn't like it. The moment of sympathy she had felt for Barnhart deflated as fast as a popped balloon. "Aren't you selling both your nephew and my sister a little short? Can't you think of another reason besides money that my sister might be interested in Luke?"

"Like what?"

"Like love, Mr. Barnhart. Or don't you believe in it?"

"Not on a month's acquaintance, I don't."

"So it's easier for you to imagine my sister is a gold digger."

Barnhart shrugged. "I don't suppose she makes much money writing kid's books."

"I make—that is L.C. makes a very good living. Next I guess you'll want to know what she means to write when she grows up, when she intends to do something more important like an adult novel."

Adam looked somewhat surprised at her ferocity. "I don't care what your sister does with her life, as long as she does it with someone besides Luke." He expelled a deep breath. "I'm sorry. I sound insulting and I don't mean it that way. We Barnhart men have learned to be a little cautious, that's all."

"Well, we Stuart women don't rob cradles or piggy banks."

"No?" he said, his eyes narrowing. "Perhaps you prefer oil shares or hotels, instead."

He was referring to those tabloid stories again. It was so unfair. The news articles held all the facts but none of the truth about the real Chelsey Stuart, the warmhearted, generous young woman, impulsive, confused, troubled in ways only Laura could understand.

"Do you always believe everything you read in the papers, Mr. Barnhart?" Laura snapped, angered on her sister's behalf.

"Shouldn't I?" he countered.

"No, you shouldn't." She met his gaze levelly, determined to make him lower his eyes, feel ashamed of himself.

But he didn't look away. She wasn't prepared for the current that suddenly seemed to rush between them, borne out of a mutual hostility, anger and an unexpected simmering of attraction. An attraction she shouldn't have been feeling. Adam Barnhart was smug, arrogant and narrow-minded.

He brought back to her, with strange clarity, an incident she had all but forgotten—the first day for her and Chelsey at their new high school. It was supposed to have been a fresh beginning after the misery and upheaval of their parents' divorce. The stone-faced principal had summoned the twins to his office first thing. With a taut smile, he had assured Laura she would not be assigned any gym or sports, but she had been enrolled in all the honors classes. They expected nothing but good things of her. As for Chelsey, the principal's smile had faded as he had growled, "We know your record and I'm informing you now, we won't tolerate your nonsense here. I have my eye on you. One false step and you'll be suspended. Is that clear, young lady?"

Chelsey had merely grinned and stuck her wad of gum to the bottom of his paperweight. It had been Laura who had been so distressed that she had had to reach for her inhaler, as ever feeling her sister's pain.

So long ago. Funny how little things had changed, Laura thought as she glared at Adam.

"Are you always this inclined to make snap judgments about people, Mr. Barnhart?" she asked bitterly.

"In my business, I often have to sum up people quickly."

"And just what is your business? Underworld spy? Corporate raider? Modern-day pirate?"

"I'm in shipping."

"Ah, a pirate, then."

"A very reluctant one," he said.

"And so you think you have me and my sister all figured out?"

"Your sister, yes, I believe so. You? I'm not so sure."

"Maybe you shouldn't make up your mind until you get to know a person better."

"Is that an invitation?"

"No! That is—what would be the point when you've already made up your mind to dislike both me and my sister?"

"Now it's you who's jumping to conclusions," he murmured. "I never said I didn't like you."

Far from it, Adam was annoyed to admit. It had been a helluva day, in which everything seemed to be falling apart, from his car, to his family, to what little bit he had managed to salvage of an old dream. And as if one Stuart woman to cut up his peace of mind had not been enough, now he had them in duplicate.

All that tension was making him feel like a heap of abandoned driftwood strewn along a beach. It would not take much more than a spark to make it ignite.

And this lady had unknowingly been providing plenty of sparks. Maybe it was because she had caught him unaware, with more than just that wild swing that had almost broken his nose. She was not in the least what he would have expected from a woman of Chelsey Stuart's reputation. The sort of female who could take up with the likes of Xavier Storm.

Adam had studied all of Mr. Storm's preferences pretty well. It was necessary with such a formidable adversary, a man who bulldozed over other people's dreams as easily as he flattened flowers and trees to lay concrete. And Storm liked his women the way he seemed to live his life—fast, bold, heedless, a little jaded.

As he observed the woman only yards from him, it occurred to Adam that Chelsey appeared to be none of those things. There was a softness and grace about her one rarely found in an independent woman these days. Maybe it was all only an illusion, a trick of the wind haloing dark curls about a face as delicate and ephemeral as moonlight. That same wind also blew her skirt, causing the folds to hug her slender hips, outline her long, willowy legs in a way to make any man grateful for the stiff breeze.

Strange he had never experienced such an attraction with her twin. But the two women were so different. The proper Miss L.C. Stuart put him off somehow with her smile, which came too quick and went too fast while never reaching her eyes.

But Chelsey had a direct way of meeting a man's gaze, even when she was frightened. Those remarkable green gold eyes, which changed to reflect her mood remained constant in one respect, ever forthright and honest.

And honesty was a quality he had learned to value in a woman, in anyone. She almost looked like the kind of person a man could tell things to, about himself, about why he was really so afraid for Luke.

But taking over the family shipping business at a young age had taught Adam a few things about revealing too much, displaying too many weaknesses, vulnerabilities. It had taken quite a few kicks in the gut, but he had learned. God, how well he had learned.

Adam realized he must have been staring too long and too hard, for Miss Stuart tensed. Her hand crept up to toy with her topmost button, and Adam found himself clenching his teeth.

Did she have any idea what that thing she kept doing with her blouse was doing to him? Who would have ever thought it could be so damned sexy watching a woman do *up* her buttons?

As she kept fidgeting with the last pearl stem, he couldn't stand it any more. He shifted his weight from the railing and closed the distance between them.

"That's not going to work," he said.

"Wh-what?" Laura breathed.

"Your buttons. You've done them up crooked."

Laura stole a hasty glance down at her blouse and was mortified to see that he was right. In her fumblings, she had skipped one of the lower buttonholes, leaving the material gapping.

Her hands flew up to correct the situation, but her fingers seemed clumsy and unsteady. Adam was standing far too close. Any nearer and the hard line of his hips would be pressed against her. Any nearer and the wall of his chest would be grazing against the whisper-thin pink silk of her blouse. Any nearer and he would have to know the crazy way her heart had begun to pound.

At least he could have had the decency to look away, but he didn't. As she struggled with the buttons, he brushed her hands impatiently aside. His fingers, strong, tanned and oddly work-callused, snagged against the sheer fabric of her blouse as he slowly eased the misplaced button back through the hole. She emitted a tiny gasp as his hand, warm and rough, grazed against her skin. She attempted to squirm away from him.

"Hold still," he said. "It's not often a pirate troubles himself to button *up* a woman's blouse."

As he moved to fasten the next button, a quiver raced through Laura. She was astonished and embarrassed to feel her nipples tighten in response as his hand brushed up against the swell of her breast.

Why was she letting him do this? she wondered in a daze. Laura knew she ought to stop him, but she felt mesmerized by the workings of that lean, strong hand, the intent expression on his face. The winter in his gray eyes turned to smoke, hot and hazy.

Things like this didn't happen to Laura Stuart, she thought wildly. She had never been cornered on a moonlit terrace by a man whose seductive mouth seemed to whisper of danger, passion, romance. And for one brief moment, she was shaken by a deep yearning for all those things, all the sweet, hot desire that Adam's lips seemed to promise. She became aware of nothing but her body's powerful physical response to this man, wanton urges, both disturbing and delicious, to melt against him.

What the hell was he doing, Adam thought a little desperately, with his hands all over Chelsey Stuart's blouse. He'd been playing Uncle Adam too damn long, had too much experience zipping up jackets and buttoning little sweaters. Except that Chelsey was no little girl. The feel of her warm skin, the taut swell of her breasts was a sharp reminder of that.

She tipped her face up toward him in a way that was both innocence and invitation, her eyes dark with longing, a longing that found an answering tug within him, as strong and deep as the pull of the tides.

Against his will, he found himself bending closer, gathering her into his arms. His lips captured hers in a tentative questing, savoring that first sample of her mouth, velvety soft.

She held herself so still for a moment, barely breathing, then she seemed to melt against him, pressing her supple body to his own hard length, sending a shaft of arousal through him. A shiver coursed through her as he made his kiss more insistent, teasing, coaxing, begging those soft lips to open for him. She surrendered with a soft sigh, enough to allow his tongue access to the moist inner recesses of her mouth.

A low moan escaped Adam as he deepened the kiss. Chelsey became all fire and sweet temptation, her tongue enticing his in a coy, seductive rhythm that was enough to steal his reason away.

This woman, so warm and vibrant in his arms, was enough to make him forget about the threat he thought her sister posed to Luke, about Chelsey Stuart's own scandalous career, the fact that she was Xavier Storm's lover.

No, that was one thing Adam could not forget.

Reluctantly, he eased his lips from hers and expelled a deep sigh.

"You know," he murmured, "I'm glad it's your sister who's been after Luke and not you."

"You are?" she whispered.

"You're a fatally attractive woman, Chelsey Stuart. Now I understand better."

"Understand what?"

"How you managed to conquer all those other men, including the redoubtable Mr. Storm. If circumstances were different, I might be tempted to add myself to the list."

Tempted to add himself—

Laura blinked, like someone who had been rudely slapped awake. The aura of romance shattered as if someone had shot out the moon. Merciful heavens, what was she doing kissing Adam Barnhart, her sister's avowed enemy?

And not just kissing him, but *kissing* him in that hot, intimate way of two lovers just before they—

Horrified, Laura thrust Adam away from her, saying in a choked voice, "No, Mr. Barnhart. That's exactly the trouble with you. You don't understand anything at all."

"Maybe not. I'm just a simple, old-fashioned guy, Miss Stuart, only interested in protecting my family. I'm going to do my best to cool off this thing between your sister and Luke."

He should worry about cooling down himself first, Laura thought, pressing a finger to her lips, still moist and tender from Adam's heated kiss.

She glared at him. "You'd better know how much I love my sister. And anyone who threatens her happiness is—is going to have to deal with me first."

"My pleasure," he growled.

"What's so pleasant?" A cheerful voice called out.

Laura's head whipped around. She was dismayed to find Luke and Chelsey strolling along the terrace. Luke regarded her and Adam with a friendly curiosity. Chelsey was the one staring, her brows arched in amazement.

How long had they been there? Laura had never heard them come out of the hotel. They must have arrived in time to see her going toe-to-toe with Adam Barnhart. Her hand snaked nervously to the collar of her blouse as Laura wondered what else they might have seen.

Before they could say anything, she began to stammer explanations. "Mr. Barnhart and I were just—just admiring the view and—and exchanging our opinions about—about family life and—and then I had something on my blouse..."

Like Adam Barnhart's hands. The hotter her face got, the more incoherent Laura became. She glanced desperately at Barnhart. Damn him! The least he could do was attempt to help her out here, instead of standing, arms folded, with that air of detached amusement.

It was Luke, sweet boy that he was, who came to her rescue.

"I'm glad you and Uncle Adam are getting along so well," he said.

"Oh, yes—yes, indeed," Laura chirped. If they were getting along any better, she and Barnhart would be shoving each other off the end of the nearest pier.

Or else making out beneath the boardwalk like a pair of lust-starved teenagers. Laura winced at the thought that popped unbidden into her head. What had gotten into her? Too much moonlight and too many buttons, she thought with a groan.

Pretending to be Chelsey was a dangerous pastime.

"It's great that you two have hit it off so well," Luke said eagerly, "because L.C. and I have come up with the best idea."

"Oh?" Laura's gaze flicked to Chelsey and she felt a flash of dread. Her sister's smile was a blend of guilt and defiance, the same way she had looked the time she had tried to get Laura out of the hospital by setting off the fire alarm.

"Our family has this beach house down the coast at Belle's Point," Luke said. "Lots of room. I spend most of the summer there and Adam comes down for weekends. So I was thinking..." Luke eyed Laura almost shyly. "Why stay here at the hotel? Since it's so late, we could all check in for the night and in the morning head down to the beach house and...spend some time there, get to know each other better."

"Luke's grandmother and sister, Jolene, would be there, too," Chelsey put in hastily, as though already sensing Laura's refusal. She slipped her arm about Laura's waist, whispering in her ear. "Please, Laura. Just two more days. You promised."

Laura didn't remember promising anything of the kind. Two more nerve-racking days of playing the part of Chelsey to a family of critical Barnharts. Spending two hot, steamy summer nights under the same roof as Adam. The next she knew, she might find him helping her with her zippers.

The notion caused a shiver to work up her spine and Laura fought off another blush. "I—I don't think we should impose—" she began.

"You and L.C. wouldn't be imposing," Luke said. "Tell them, Uncle Adam."

Adam appeared to like the idea even less than Laura did. A tiny frown had settled between his eyes. "Don't pressure Miss Stuart, Luke," he said. "I think she'd be bored at Belle's Point. No casinos, no nightclubs, not exactly the sort of wild nightlife she's used to."

It was obvious he didn't want Laura or Chelsey coming to his family home. At any other time, such a rebuff would have sent Laura scurrying in the opposite direction. But something about Adam Barnhart roused a streak of resistance in her, a perversity Laura had never known she possessed.

"I think I could dispense with my wild nightlife for a few days," she said sweetly. "A quiet weekend by the shore sounds wonderful."

"Of course, the mosquitoes on the cape are bad this time of year," Adam said. "We've also had a shark sighting recently, and then there are the storms—"

"Adam!" Luke protested, half laughing, half reproachful. "You're going to make Chelsey and L.C. think they're not welcome."

Adam gave a thin smile. "No, I only wanted to warn them what they might be getting into."

But Laura felt the warning was mostly for her. There was a challenge in Adam's eyes as hot and heavy as the kiss they had shared. It fired her blood, filled her with a strange feeling of recklessness.

Smiling at Luke, Laura said, "It was kind of you to invite us, Luke. L.C. and I would be happy to come."

Luke beamed, and Chelsey gave a happy squeal, hugging Laura. Over Chelsey's shoulder, Laura met Adam's gaze.

His eyes like molten steel, he nodded as if conceding the first round to her. But as he turned to walk away, Laura was left with the sensation of teetering on the brink of some storm-ridden cliff, a sensation that was as exhilarating as it was terrifying.

Laura would persuade Chelsey to tell Luke the truth. This masquerade would only continue for two more days, she reassured herself.

Why, then, did she have the feeling she was about to embark on the longest weekend of her life?

Three

What fool ever said that things always looked brighter in the morning? Adam wondered, gritting his teeth. The white Italian sports car bucked like an angry mule as he attempted to ease it out of the slot in the hotel's parking garage. He popped the clutch and the motor stalled. Muttering a curse, he vowed that the next time he borrowed a car, he'd make damned sure it was an automatic. Shifting into neutral, he attempted to start the convertible again.

He'd grown well past the age of lusting after a flashy vehicle, which folded his knees up to his chin for the sake of being able to do a hundred miles over the legal speed limit. He preferred his own luxury sedan, which did the job of transferring him from one sales meeting to the next in comfort and style. That seemed to be the sum total of his life these days.

He wondered when he'd gotten so—so middle-aged in his views, a condition he'd only recently become aware of while watching Luke in the throes of his first romance. Adam had always tried to be more friend than guardian to his nephew, or at least so he'd thought. But lately, Luke seemed to be regarding Adam as something of an "old fogy." Adam suspected the prim Miss L.C. Stuart was responsible for the wedge being driven between himself and Luke.

Other times he feared it might be his own fault for being so impatient and critical of Luke's infatuation. Adam knew his brother would have handled the situation better. Flashing his easygoing grin, Jack had always handled everything better, from running Barnhart Shipping to drying his toddlers' tears when they took a tumble. Only Jack's kids weren't toddlers any more, and Jack wasn't here.

Adam gripped the steering wheel hard for a moment, flooded with the familiar pain and regret even after twelve years. He had to force himself to put Jack from his mind, concentrate on Jack's son, Luke.

He was going to have to try being at least a little bit sympathetic about Luke's fling with this children's book author. Trouble was, Adam had almost forgotten what it was like to be that bowled over by any woman.

At least until last night.

Adam tried to sweep the irritating thought aside, determined not to dwell upon that hot kiss between himself and Chelsey Stuart on the terrace, dismissing it as of no importance.

Hormones, he reassured himself as he eased down his foot on the accelerator. This time he managed to get the car backed all the way out before stalling again.

Nothing but rampant hormones. He compressed his lips and twisted the keys in the ignition. And it was all the more disgusting because he was no longer some college-age male with libido for brains.

He wasn't the sort to be all over a woman he'd just met, especially not one such as Chelsey Stuart. Damned, irritating female. If he crinkled his nose, he could still feel the bruise her suitcase had left. As well as recall some of the things she had said to him, trying to make him feel as if he were some narrow-minded, overbearing tyrant, as if he were the one who was wrong about Luke and L.C.

Adam had been president of a corporation since he was Luke's age and the head of a family for equally as long. He wasn't accustomed to having his judgment called into question. Though he hated to admit it, he had a certain grudging respect for Chelsey standing up to him, for defending her sister. If anybody could appreciate family loyalty, it was him.

But admiration of Chelsey Stuart's—er—family virtues was not enough to account for the jolt of attraction that had sizzled between them. One look into Chelsey's large, liquid eyes and he'd felt like a man pulled away by a strong undertow. Before he'd known where he was at, he'd been kissing her, his mind filling with images of playing out beach scenes like in *From Here to Eternity.*

Him. The man who'd never made love to a woman anywhere except in the comfort of a bed.

The notion brought a self-mocking smile to his lips, the first one since he'd gotten up that morning. He never slept well in hotels, and knowing that this one was just another facet of Storm Enterprises hadn't made it any easier. Adam had looked about him to criticize, find some structural flaw, but there hadn't been any. Everything at the Sea King was slick, expensive and luxurious. A fine place to stay if you like a lot of chrome, glass and modern decor as sterile as a hospital. Adam didn't.

As he guided the car out of the garage into the bright light of day, his mood didn't improve when he found the turnaround in front of the hotel blocked.

One of those roving television minivans and a station wagon from some news agency had been left parked in the yellow curb zone. The sidewalk leading to the hotel entrance was thronged with reporters and photographers.

Muttering a curse, Adam started to back up with only an idle passing thought for what was going on. Had some movie star arrived or, God forbid, maybe even Storm himself making one of his calculated public appearances.

Adam tramped down hard on the brake as he suddenly caught sight of a familiar figure trying to fight her way through the swarm of reporters. Laura Stuart used the sheen of her soft brown hair as an ineffective shield against the microphones being shoved at her, the flash of camera bulbs. When she glanced up, looking desperately for some avenue of escape, Adam saw her panic-stricken expression, like a roe deer at bay amid a pack of snarling wolves.

He didn't pause to think or weigh consequences. He only reacted. Shifting gears, for once the sports car responded to his touch like a fiery stallion ready to charge into action. Adam turned the wheel and hit the gas, sending the car around the minivan, bounding up over the curb onto the sidewalk.

The roar of the motor and the squeal of the tires momentarily caused the startled press hounds to fall back. Leaning across the seat, Adam flung open the passenger-side door.

"Get in," he bellowed at Laura, who was still pretending to be Chelsey.

She gaped at him for a moment, then with a grateful gasp staggered toward the car, almost hurling herself inside. Even as she yanked the door closed, some of the reporters were pressing against the glass, still shouting questions.

"Miss Stuart. Will you testify at the Storm divorce trial?"

"Any truth to the story you and Storm have a love nest in Paris?"

"What about the rumor you took naked photos of Storm for *She* magazine?"

The sound of their voices faded as Adam sent the car bouncing off the curb. He whipped the vehicle out into the flow of street traffic. Ignoring the blare of horns, he took off, recklessly weaving in and out of the cars ahead as if being hotly pursued.

He felt strangely exhilarated, for once able to appreciate the car's power. He never drove this way. He'd always been too busy setting a good example for his nephew and niece.

It wasn't until he whipped around a black-and-white squad car that he came to his senses. Figuring he'd put a safe distance between the woman at his side and the mob at the hotel, he pulled over to the curb, parking before a quaint summer boardinghouse with a blue-and-white awning.

Turning to his passenger, he found her clutching the sides of her leather-upholstered seat. She was white and trembling, whether from his driving at her recent brush with the press, Adam couldn't tell.

"Are you all right?" he asked.

She nodded, but when she tried to speak, it was in halting breaths. "It's only—all so unexpected. When I came into the lobby— Were waiting for me. Of—of course I'm usually quite accustomed to—to dealing with the press."

She didn't seem accustomed to anything. Rather she looked more like she was about to go into shock. Adam had a volatile mother and a teenage niece, and comforting distraught females had become practically second nature to him.

Scarcely thinking what he was doing, he leaned closer, slipping his hand beneath Laura's hair to massage the satiny smooth skin at the nape of her neck.

"Close your eyes," he said. "Take deep breaths."

She did as he commanded, nestling further back against the warm strength of Adam's soothing fingers.

She was not off to a very good start this morning, Laura thought ruefully. She feared she'd blown her impersonation of Chelsey already, as soon as she'd stepped off the elevator into an ambush of reporters.

Just another little surprise, a side effect of being Chelsey Stuart that her sister had neglected to warn Laura about. She had tried to handle them with Chelsey's breezy aplomb. But they had closed in on Laura, their rapid-fire questions sounding so hard and hostile, camera flashes going off in her eyes like miniature explosions.

She'd abandoned pieces of her luggage across the lobby in her efforts to escape, but the reporters and photographers had hounded her all the way to the sidewalk outside the hotel. She had begun to get the old panicky sensation of her air being cut off that she had always associated with her childhood asthma attacks. Even though she knew she was fine, she would have welcomed the comforting feel of an inhaler clutched in her hand.

But Adam's hand seemed to be doing just as well, the slightly callused pads of his fingertips abrading her neck in slow, sensual swirls, sending tingles of warmth rushing through her.

Then she made the mistake of opening her eyes and found herself staring straight into his compelling gray ones. She became suddenly aware that a sports car was much too small for a man of Adam's masculine proportions, the broad shoulders and long, rangy legs.

They were crammed too close together, only the stick-shift console between them. The warmth Adam's fingers were sending through Laura became a flush of heat, and she felt that same disconcerting pulse beat of attraction for this man. Her sister's adversary. And this time Laura didn't even have the moonlight to blame it on.

Dismayed, she disengaged his hand and thrust it firmly away from her. "Th-thank you. I'm fine now. I didn't mean to behave like a hysterical idiot. It's just—"

"I understand," he interrupted. "I'm a private person myself. When a camera gets thrust at me, I act like a savage afraid someone's out to steal bits of my soul."

Out to steal bits of her soul. Yes, that's exactly what it had felt like. Laura blinked, amazed by Adam's empathy and perception. It was the last comment she would have expected from a hardheaded, practical person like him.

She almost warmed to the man until he continued, "Though I never imagined that *you* would be the same. Frankly, you've always struck me as being the sort of woman who welcomes publicity."

So he was back to that again, more critical hints about Chelsey's tabloid career.

Laura stiffened. "You thought that I would actually like being in the center of a media circus?"

"Yes, I guess I did," he confessed. His eyes narrowed with more puzzlement than suspicion. "I certainly never figured you for the camera-shy type."

After the fright she'd just had, the distress found release in a surge of anger. "Oh, no, Mr. Barnhart, I just adore having cameras shoved in my face and being asked a hundred impertinent questions."

"Impertinent?" His lips quirked in a half smile.

Oh, God, she was doing it again. Talking like a character out of a Jane Austen novel. The realization of her slipup did nothing to soothe Laura's exacerbated feelings.

"Nosy questions," she corrected, glaring at him. "And if you think I was enjoying myself back there—"

"Whoa! If I had thought you were enjoying yourself, I never would have come to your rescue."

"I'm astonished you did. After some of the things you said to me last night, I would have thought you'd be more inclined to use me for shark bait."

"That notion did occur to me," he said dryly. "But I've always been a sucker for a damsel in distress. Even when I don't get so much as a thank-you."

"Excuse me, but I never asked you to come roaring up like—like James Bond in your little gadget car."

"In this case, the little gadget car belongs to James Bond's mother. This kind of sporty vehicle is not exactly my style."

"*You* have a mother?"

"Contrary to what you might think, I didn't crawl out from under a rock."

"I didn't mean— It's only that my mother drives a station wagon and I wouldn't have thought— Oh, never mind." Leaning back in her seat, Laura blew out a gust of air, dismayed by how quickly Adam Barnhart was able to get her irritated and flustered.

"Look, Miss Stuart, this is nothing for us to get into another argument about," he said. "I wasn't trying to offend you. All I mean is that you surprised me. Any woman who is a—er—a good friend of Xavier Storm's has to expect this kind of publicity. If you don't like it, maybe you should reconsider the company you keep."

"Maybe I should, Mr. Barnhart," she said with acid sweetness, staring straight at him.

But he didn't seem to get the point of her remark. He was too busy staring himself, his eyes drifting downward, subjecting her to a slow, lingering once-over that made her skin tingle.

"I can hardly blame those fellows back there for wanting to take your picture. That's quite an outfit you're wearing."

Self-consciously, Laura tried to tug her hemline down past mid-thigh. A hopeless task. There was more material in an infant's receiving blanket than in this knit skirt of Chelsey's. And the hot pink ribbed tank top strained so tight across her breasts, the lacing tended to gap a little, revealing hints of creamy white skin. The formfitting top didn't leave room for the modesty of a bra beneath.

"I haven't seen skirts that short since the mini craze when I was in junior high," Adam murmured.

Laura raised her chin defensively. "I've always been into nostalgia," she said, thinking of her closetful of romantic Laura Ashley dresses and Victorian blouses.

"All you need is the fishnet stockings."

"All I need is a taxi cab to take me back to the hotel," she snapped.

"Hotel?" The half-mocking glimmer that had been in his eyes darkened as he frowned. "But what about the reporters? They might still be there."

"I'll take my chances. I left my luggage strewn all over the lobby, and my sister will wonder what happened to me."

"That can easily be taken care of."

Adam's arm shot out and Laura gave a soft squeak of alarm. But he was only reaching beneath the dash and extracting . . . a car phone.

Laura knew she was out of step with the nineties, but she had never used such a thing before. Even her fiancé—her ex-fiancé—had never owned one, and it might have come in handy with Tom's medical practice.

She watched with reluctant fascination as Adam punched up the local operator and got the number of the hotel. Ringing the lobby, he ordered them to page Luke Barnhart and Miss L.C. Stuart.

With his usual high-handedness, he told his nephew what had happened and began barking out orders. "You and L.C. gather up the luggage and turn in Miss Stuart's rental car. When I think it's safe, we'll meet you at the back entrance of the hotel. What? Oh." Adam extended the receiver to Laura in an impatient gesture. "Your sister wants to talk to you."

Laura accepted the phone gingerly as if half fearing it might explode. She lifted the receiver to her ear. "Hello?"

"Hi, kiddo!" Chelsey's voice sounded entirely too perky. "So, I hear you had a little adventure."

"Yes." Laura gritted her teeth into a smile for Adam's sake. "You might have warned me."

"Hey, I told you I didn't think it was a good idea that you signed your name as Chelsey Stuart in the hotel register."

But I'm supposed to be you. Who else should I have signed in as, Madonna? It was all Laura could do to choke back the indignant words.

"One of the hotel clerks probably sold you out to the press for a nice fat tip. But Uncle Adam came to the rescue, and I doubt they'll track us to Belle's Point, so no harm done."

Laura could picture Chelsey shrugging, already dismissing the harrowing incident.

"Actually, this all worked out perfectly, hon."

"Perfectly embarrassing," Laura muttered.

"No, I mean it. Now Uncle Adam can drive you down to the cape. It'll give you another chance to be alone with him."

"I don't want another chance to—" Catching Adam staring, Laura lowered her tone and forced the sticky sweet smile back to her lips. "I don't think that's a good idea, L.C."

"Sure it is. It'll give you a chance to work on him about accepting me and Luke, soften him up for me."

Laura stole a nervous glance at the hard angles of Adam's profile, that uncompromising set to his lips, the formidable outline of his granitelike shoulders. Soften him up? She'd need a baseball bat.

She started to protest, but Chelsey rushed on breathlessly, "Gotta run. Luke will be bringing the car round. We'll leave at once. See you at the beach house. Bye."

"Chel—L.C.!" But Laura's only response was a discordant click, followed by the ominous hum of disconnection. She handed the phone back to Adam with a sinking heart, scarcely able to meet his eyes.

"Well?" he asked, appearing to sense that something was wrong.

"Uh, L.C. said she and Luke are heading out with my luggage. They'll meet us at the beach house. I'm all checked out. She—she figured you could drive me."

"Did she?" Adam's quick frown revealed he was little better pleased with the situation than Laura.

"How *impertinent* of her," he drawled.

That did it. Laura was not going to drive an inch farther, stuffed inside this lilliputian sports car with this overbearing hunk of a man who was too sarcastic and far too handy with a lady's buttons.

She yanked at the door handle. "I certainly don't intend to inconvenience you, Mr. Barnhart. I'm sure I'll have no difficulty in flagging down a bus."

"More likely you'll cause an accident. Any red-blooded male would slam on the brakes for you wearing that skirt."

Her cheeks flaming, Laura shoved the car door open. But Adam reached across her in time to grab the handle. He practically had her pinned to the seat, the solid, muscular length of his arm acting as a barricade to her escape. The movement brought his face closer to her own. She caught a whiff of his after-shave, reminding her of the scent and the taste of him last night when he'd kissed her all but senseless. Her heart skittered a wild beat.

"Forget it, Miss Stuart," he said. "I can't have you wreaking havoc with the local traffic. It's bad enough." He managed to tug the door closed. "I'll drive you to the cape. After all, you are my guest."

"A guest who's not welcome. You've made that abundantly clear."

"Look, I know we have our differences, a lot of them. But we're going to be spending the weekend together. Maybe we should declare a truce."

"What kind of truce?" she asked warily. "You mean like starting all over again from last night?"

"Now that's a tempting thought, but not a wise one." He was twisted on his seat, his arms braced on either side of her as if he still expected her to make a bolt for it. The front of his shirt brushed against the swell of her breast, the cool, crisp fabric tickling her exposed skin. She saw the rise and fall of his chest as his gaze came to rest upon her mouth.

It was obvious he felt it, too, this crazy push-pull of attraction that shouldn't exist. This unexpected current running between two people determined to dislike each other, whose interests were totally opposed.

"Why did you kiss me last night?" she blurted out, and then was appalled. It was the last thing she wanted to bring up at this particular moment.

"I don't know," he growled, his eyes mirroring her own confusion. "But damn it, I keep wanting more."

Laura started to protest as Adam's head dipped lower, but his mouth was already on hers, hot and seeking as if demanding the answer to her question with all of his usual, hard impatience.

The heel of her hand jammed against his shoulder as she tried to resist, but she already felt her first quiver of response. Her lips seemed to part before his onslaught, as if her mouth had been formed for the sole purpose of melding with his.

His tongue delved inside, mating with hers in a slow, provocative rhythm, sending heat rippling through her like thermal waves from a pavement on a sweltering day. Adam tried to pull her closer, cupping his hand behind her knee. The heat of his palm seemed to scorch through her nylon, sending warmth flooding to settle in a heavy, aching pool between her thighs.

A soft moan caught in Laura's throat. Every instinct she possessed urged her to press her body to his, an impossible feat with a gearshift between them. There was not even room in this blasted sports car to allow a woman to go suitably weak in the knees.

Adam wrenched his mouth from hers, his eyes dark with frustration. "There!" he said huskily, his voice almost angry. "I hope that answers your question."

Laura couldn't even remember what it was. She sagged back in her seat, dazed by her own passionate response as much as Adam's. It would not have surprised her to discover the car windows were steamed.

Adam flung himself to the driver's side, his breath coming quick and shallow. He nearly yanked the seat belt out of its socket as he fastened it across his chest with a sharp click.

As Laura struggled to fasten her own with trembling fingers, she had an urge to break into hysterical laughter. Motor companies didn't make safety devices for the kind of danger that pulsed between her and Adam.

"This is your idea of a truce, Mr. Barnhart?" she managed to gasp at last.

"Yeah, and you have to admit—" he drew in a ragged breath "—it's a helluva improvement over détente." His glare suddenly dissolved into a reluctant grin. "And under the circumstances, Miss Stuart, I think you better start calling me by my first name."

"Uncle Adam?"

"Just plain Adam will do." His smile for once was genuine, lighting up all the way to his eyes. Astonishing what a difference it made, softening the harsh cast of his features, making even the faint trace of his chin scar seem less menacing.

"And you can call me L—" Laura caught herself just in time. "Call me Chelsey," she finished glumly.

She was suddenly faced with a new and unwelcome complication to this impersonation. She tried to tell herself that the first passionate kiss she had shared with Adam was the product of moonlight and imagination, romantic sea breezes and starry skies.

But now in glaring daylight, cramped into bucket seats with a gearshift stuck between them, the magic of the desire was still there.

And she couldn't even tell him her real name. But there was one bit of the truth she could offer him, and it suddenly seemed vitally important to Laura that she do so.

"Adam," she said, "I—I just want you to know. No matter what the newspapers say, I'm not any man's...good friend. Especially not Xavier Storm's."

He betrayed no response, not even the flicker of an eyelash. But as Adam reached to turn on the ignition, she thought she heard him say softly, "Good. I'm glad."

Four

The brisk sea wind tangled Laura's hair in her eyes as the convertible sped along the old seacoast road. Somewhere in a little town called Marmora, Adam had stopped for gas and put the top down. The rush of air, the dizzying blue of the sky overhead made Laura feel almost breathless.

Tossing her hair back, she reflected on strange twists of fate and Chelsey. In Laura's experience, the two had often amounted to the same thing. She had come to the shore to visit her sister on a simple vacation. Now here she was zooming along in a sports car, wearing a miniskirt, her mouth still tender from having been kissed by a hard-eyed pirate of a man with sun-streaked hair and a sinister scar on his chin—a man who might be likely to strangle her when he discovered the deception she was practicing.

It was crazy. It was frightening. It was strangely exhilarating. If this wasn't an adventure, it was as close as Laura Stuart ever expected to get to one.

Resting one sinewy forearm on the window ledge, Adam squinted against the glare on the windshield, causing leathery lines to feather out around his eyes. He kept his concentration fixed on the road ahead, but from time to time his gaze would flick her way and he would squirm in his seat.

"We're almost to Belle's Point," he said above the rush of the wind. "From there it's only a short leg—er—short way to the beach house."

Laura nodded, aware of what kept pulling Adam's focus. But she couldn't do anything about it. The fabric of that skirt just wouldn't give another inch and there was no place to put long legs such as hers in a sports car, except tilted toward the gearshift.

Adam expelled a deep breath, moistened his lips and fidgeted with the mile counter. Soften him up, Chelsey had told Laura. Laura was afraid that was not the effect she was having on the man.

Shame on you, Laura, she chided herself. She didn't inspire men to a state of spontaneous arousal, or at least not that she had ever noticed. She supposed that if she had any real sex appeal, she would never have caught her ex-fiancé behind the filing cabinets with his secretary.

But the simmering attraction in Adam's eyes made her feel sultry, seductive and irresistible. She knew he was only responding to her borrowed plumes as Chelsey and that this absurd masquerade would have to end soon enough. But was it so wrong of her, Laura thought wistfully, to enjoy it just a little bit in the meantime?

Especially now that she had discovered Adam could be human, almost charming. When he wasn't being distracted by her legs, he pointed out places of interest in the little inland towns they passed through, regaled her with some of the quaint local lore. Laura knew she ought to bring up the matter of her sister's relationship with Luke, try to plead

Chelsey's cause. But somehow she couldn't bring herself to mention anything that might shatter the tentative harmony between herself and Adam.

Before she realized it, they were closing in on their destination.

"That's Belle's Point dead ahead," he said. "Don't blink your eyes or you're going to miss it."

The car hummed over a small span of steel bridge, and Adam was obliged to slow down as they reached the town limits. Laura saw a typical sleepy fishing village, with its clapboard houses, a few shops, the spire of a church, the gas station with its requisite cola machine and live-bait dispenser. What passed for the main street ended at a tiny harbor and pier, a variety of pleasure craft and fishing boats docked in boat slips.

Adam slowed so Laura could have a better look at the marina. "That was the site of the first Barnhart shipyard before the business was moved to Philadelphia. They say my great-grandfather used to build fishing sloops by day and practice a little backwater piracy by night."

"And does the current president keep up the family tradition?" Laura asked.

"No, he attends production meetings, studies sales figures and fields a lot of phone calls." Adam's tone was so flat and unenthusiastic, Laura stared at him.

Her curious regard seemed to prod him into adding, "I guess modern-day piracy isn't nearly as exciting, or maybe I'm just not that good at it. Your friend—that is, Mr. Storm is probably a lot better."

"Do you know Storm?"

"As much as I care to."

"And you don't like him very much?"

"Let's just say we have our differences."

"Like us?"

"No, I've never had an urge to kiss Storm," he retorted with a grin. He was quick to change the subject to the story of some ancient shipwreck as he guided the car out of town. Laura was left with the distinct impression that Adam was not at ease discussing Storm with her, that he still did not quite trust her.

And he had no reason to, Laura reflected. She was deceiving him with practically every word that came out of her mouth. The thought was not a comfortable one, and she tried to put it out of her head. Conscience pangs didn't seem to go too well with having adventures.

And suddenly she wasn't anxious for this one to end. The car whizzed past a sweep of coast that was beautiful, the houses falling away to leave nothing but sandy shore, even the rolling Atlantic looking benign and sunlit today.

All too soon, Adam halted the car on a concrete drive leading up to the Barnhart's beach house. The house itself was perched above on a rocky outcropping of land. Tilting her head back, Laura gaped up at it. She didn't know what she'd been expecting when Luke had talked of the beach house, but certainly nothing like this structure, straight out of the pages of a guide to modern architecture.

In her amazement, she scrambled up the seat, craning her neck for a better view. It looked like a gigantic sand dune, the sea-facing wall angling down in tiers of glass. Busy staring, it took her a moment to realize that Adam had gotten out of the car and come round to lean against the passenger-side door.

"The Barnhart *hacienda,*" he said with a sweeping gesture. "So what do you think?"

"It's—it's very modern," Laura said.

"I'm not crazy about it, either." He pulled a rueful face. "The old house that we had here was more cozy, not much more than a fisherman's cottage. But it got washed out to sea."

"Washed out to sea?" Laura echoed weakly. She twisted around to glance back toward the distant outline of the ocean, which no longer seemed quite so benign.

Adam laughed. "During the hurricane in '62. But don't look so worried. I can personally assure you that this house isn't going anywhere."

Before Laura could guess what he meant to do, he suddenly dipped down and got his arm beneath her knees, scooping her out of the sports car. Startled, Laura flung her arms around his neck in a gesture of pure instinct.

For a moment, she was cradled high against his chest, staring at those sea gray eyes, the sensual curve of his mouth. Her heart slammed against her ribs as he lowered her slowly to her feet. She slid down the length of him, aware of every hard contour of his frame, the heat, the vitality that seemed to radiate from the man.

"What was wrong with the door?" she managed to say a little breathlessly.

"Nothing. Just call it another of those crazy impulses that seem to keep coming over me since I've met you, Chelsey Stuart."

She fully understood what he meant. She was having another impulse herself, conscious of how well her softer curves fit against him, conscious of her desire to stay where she was, within the circle of his arms.

This had to stop. Placing one hand against his chest, she levered herself back a step. "I—I wonder where Luke and L.C. are. I don't see Luke's car."

It was an unfortunate reminder. That smoky look vanished from Adam's eyes as he glanced up the drive with a frown.

"They should be here by now. They had a head start on us and . . . and I didn't come by the most direct route."

That was an interesting confession, and Adam looked a little sheepish making it. Laura couldn't help wondering, had he done so to spend more time with her or did Adam just like a scenic view?

"I am sure nothing is wrong," she said. "I have the impression that Luke must be a very careful driver."

"It's not Luke's driving that I'm worried about."

"Well, my sister didn't kidnap him or anything like that, either."

"No?" Adam quirked one brow at her. "I have your word for that?"

Laura started to nod, then hesitated. No one could ever give assurance of what Chelsey Stuart might take it into her head to do next. Instead, Laura said, "I'm sure your nephew is old enough to take care of himself. I know you still think of yourself as his guardian, but it can't be good for either of you, hovering over him the way you do."

She wasn't sure how Adam would take the criticism, but all he said was, "And I suppose you're an expert on how a guardian should behave."

"No, only on overprotection," she said sadly and then cringed, realizing that she had broken character, slipping back into Laura again. He dusted one fingertip, lightly, gently across the bridge of her nose.

"Funny. Sometimes you look like you could take on the whole seventh fleet. And other times you look as though you need some protecting yourself." The expression in his eyes became almost tender. Then he seemed to give himself a mental shake. "At least some protection from the sun. Come on. I better get you in the house. I think your nose is starting to blister."

Laura wouldn't have been at all surprised. She'd been so busy working on the book, she hadn't poked her nose out-of-doors much this past month. With her hand locked in his, Adam led her up the steep flagstone steps that stretched up to the front door.

He tried the handle, then fished out his key. "Nobody's home. My mother must be out shopping. I forgot to tell you we're having a small party tonight."

"Party?" Laura asked with a tingle of unease.

"Nothing major. Only a hundred or so of my mother's most intimate friends."

"A hundred!" The tingle became a full-scale five alarm.

"Just kidding," Adam grinned as he shoved the front door open. "Actually, it will only be a few people from Belle's Point. I'm sure they'll all be dying to meet you, Chelsey."

"I'll bet," Laura muttered. She hadn't counted on anything such as this. It seemed to her that the larger the crowd she attempted to play out this charade with, the more she risked slipping up and exposing herself.

Now it was her turn to peer anxiously back down the road for some sign of her sister and Luke.

"Oh, Chelsey," she murmured as she trailed Adam into the house. "Help!"

Unfortunately, the only help Chelsey provided when she did arrive was to lay out Laura's dress for the party. While Laura was showering, Chelsey did a quick sneak into the room they were sharing at the beach house, changed her own clothes and disappeared. Laura had the distinct feeling Chelsey was trying to avoid being alone with her, and it wasn't a comforting notion.

She was left with no choice but to make her appearance at the party as Chelsey Stuart. As Laura hovered on the threshold of the living room that dominated the beach house, she saw that the number of guests only amounted to about thirty. But that was daunting enough.

Laura had never enjoyed large parties, especially when she didn't know most of the people present. It was even worse when she was having an identity crisis.

She was still introverted Laura, but she was wearing one of Chelsey's most extroverted outfits, a slinky off-the-shoulder cocktail dress of flaming red, the silken material swishing seductively about her hips. It was like a blinking neon sign, drawing every gaze in the room toward her, especially those of the men.

Trying not to look too self-conscious, Laura minced down into the sunken living room, hoping she wouldn't stumble and fall flat on her face. These heels of Chelsey's, which matched the dress, were high enough to give you a nosebleed. The pointed toes crushed her as tightly as the ancient Chinese practice of binding women's feet. No pain, no gain, was Chelsey's philosophy, even in shoes. If they didn't pinch like hell, they couldn't possibly be sexy.

Laura thought she could have done with a little less sex appeal and a lot more comfort. She limped as far as the chrome-and-glass built-in bar and paused, feeling awkward and alone. There was a balding man over by the stone fireplace who was actually leering at her.

When Adam suddenly loomed in front of her, Laura breathed a tiny sigh of relief. Sleeping Beauty couldn't have been more glad to see her prince riding to the rescue. Although in this case the prince was wearing slacks and a casual knit shirt opened at the neck to expose an intriguing vee of sun-bronzed skin. With his ash blond hair swept back from his brow, he looked as rugged and weather-beaten as a sailor home from the sea. His storm gray eyes skated over Laura with a warm appreciation.

"So this evening we have the lady in red," he murmured.

"More like the scarlet woman." Laura fidgeted with the thin gold chain about her neck. "Please tell me I'm just being paranoid and everyone is not really gaping at me."

Adam pulled a face. "I'm afraid we're both a little notorious." He directed her attention to a folded newspaper on top of the bar, one of the local scandal sheets.

Laura's heart sank as she saw the photographers from that morning hadn't wasted any time. Not only was there a picture of her fleeing the Sea King Hotel, there was also a shot of her roaring off in the sports car. Apparently some enterprising reporter had been able to identify the driver, for the coy caption read, "Storm and Barnhart Contesting More than Beachfront Property?"

Laura didn't understand the reference to beachfront property, but the other innuendo was clear enough. Storm and Adam were now thought to be fighting over her—or rather Chelsey. Laura cringed, remembering all that Adam had said about liking his privacy and hating publicity.

"Oh, Adam, I—I don't know what to say," she said, biting down upon her lip.

Adam shrugged and folded up the newspaper. "I guess it's the price one pays for playing James Bond."

And Chelsey Stuart, Laura thought ruefully.

"I'm so sorry—" she began, but was cut off by a throaty female voice.

"There's nothing to apologize for, dear. Actually, it's a very good photo of my car. I'm thinking of having it framed."

Laura turned to find a diminutive bird of a woman pressed close to her elbow. Dressed in a beaded jumpsuit, she had short-cropped hair bleached almost white and eyes the same deep gray as Adam's. Laura was left with no doubt about her identity.

So this was James Bond's mother, the owner of the flashy white sports car. Laura regarded her with dazed fascination as Adam performed the introductions.

"Chelsey, this is my mother, Louise Barnhart. Lou, this is Miss Chelsey Stuart."

Lou. He called his mother Lou, and she was wearing earrings shaped like tiny dice with diamond studs for the dots. Laura's own mother had been more the June Cleaver variety, discreet pearls worn to match her aprons and sedate housedresses.

But there was genuine warmth in Louise Barnhart's eyes as she stood on tiptoe to give Laura a peck on the cheek. "Chelsey, so sorry I wasn't here to greet you when you arrived. It's been hectic getting ready for the party, but I'm glad you could join us for the weekend. It's been too long since Adam brought a young lady home."

"Oh, I'm not—" Laura spluttered. "That is, he didn't exactly bring me."

"You walked?" Lou asked.

"No, Adam drove me here in your car, but he didn't—"

"Then he brought you," Lou said firmly, as if that were the end of the matter.

Laura writhed in embarrassment, hoping Adam would clear up his mother's misconception. But he merely folded his arms, looking amused.

"Now, Chelsey, if there's anything you need this weekend, you just ask," Louise said, patting her arm. "There's a lovely pool out back. Adam had it put in to please my grandchildren. Are you fond of children, Chelsey?"

"Subtle, Lou. Very subtle," Adam muttered darkly.

But Louise blithely ignored him. "Of course, you must be fond of children with all those charming books you write for them."

Laura gave such a start, she nearly tumbled off her heels.

"That's the other sister, Lou," Adam said. "The one who came with Luke."

Laura's heart almost resumed a normal beat until he added, "Chelsey's job is photographing naked men."

The man was an absolute devil. Before Laura could stammer out a disclaimer, Louise clapped her hands and exclaimed. "My God, how delightful. You must show me some of your work. Now come along and I'll introduce you to my card club."

"Oh, yes," Laura said with a weak smile. "My mother used to play bridge, too."

"Bridge?" Lou gave a snort of laughter. "Poker, dear. Five-card stud and deuces wild."

She propelled Laura away like a miniature tornado, only allowing Laura a second to glance back and shoot Adam a blistering glance. He merely leaned against the bar and raised a glass in mocking salute.

Meeting the Barnharts' guests was not the ordeal Laura had feared. Although most of them eyed her as if she were some exotic fan dancer, they were friendly enough, especially the men. By the time Laura had made a full circuit of the room, she had an invitation to go waterskiing, an offer to channel her past lives and a coupon for a free exam at a podiatrist's. Considering the way Chelsey's heels were crucifying her feet, Laura had a feeling she was going to need it.

The only people present that Laura found she actually disliked were the Drs. Leaming, a pair of married dentists. Dr. Leaming was the balding man who had leered at her earlier, and from the way he kept ogling Laura didn't think it was her teeth that excited his admiration. But the man's wife all but took him by the ear to haul him away from her, leaving Laura to the mercy of the couple's teenage son.

Chad Leaming had short, spiked black hair and perfect capped teeth, no doubt courtesy of Mom and Dad. His idea of party attire appeared to be a black leather jacket, jeans torn in interesting places and a dangling earring shaped like a skull. His idea of party conversation consisted of corralling Laura in a corner and calling her "babe."

"So, babe," he said, bracing one arm against the wall beside her. "I saw your picture in the paper."

Laura wrinkled her nose, trying not to sneeze at the assault of his heavy cologne. "So did everyone else in South Jersey, I imagine."

He gave her a broad wink. "But I think we've got a mutual friend."

"I doubt it." She didn't recall having any acquaintances numbered among the rejects from Hell's Angels. Laura tried to duck past Chad, but he blocked her path.

"Hey, babe, just trying to be friendly. This party is practically dead. What say we—"

"Beat it, junior," Chelsey interrupted, striding up with a breezy smile. "Your mama wants you."

Chad turned brick red and looked discomfited, especially since it was true. His mother was beckoning to him from the other side of the room. His macho stride somewhat chastened, he slunk off with a sulky scowl.

"I could've handled that, Chelsey," Laura said in low tones.

"Sure you could, kiddo."

Laura didn't know what irritated her more. Chelsey's patronizing attitude or the fact that her sister was wearing those fake glasses again, the wire-rims perched on the end of her nose.

Under the pretext of admiring Laura's gold chain, Chelsey leaned close enough to whisper, "Lighten up, Laura. You're way too tense."

"You would be too if that little weasel had been trying to look down the front of your dress."

"Then avoid him. Circulate. I have a reputation for being livelier at parties."

"If you don't like the way I'm playing you, get someone else for the part," Laura snapped. "Are you any closer to telling Luke the truth?"

Chelsey regarded her with large, wounded eyes. "Cut me some slack, hon. We just got here. It's only Friday night. I have all weekend to break the news."

When Laura glowered at her, Chelsey backed off, saying, "What you need is a drink. I'll go fix you one."

"No, thank you—"

"Something harmless, I swear." Chelsey flashed a bright grin. "Some Long Island tea, perhaps."

Laura fumed as she watched her sister work her way back through the crowd to the bar. Even though Laura had promised Chelsey the weekend, she had hoped that Chelsey might have settled things with Luke by now. Laura should have known better. Chelsey had a bad habit of avoiding anything unpleasant for as long as possible. Laura would have to turn up the pressure on her sister. The longer this masquerade went on, the more embarrassing and awkward it seemed to get.

But she felt a little better when Chelsey brought her the drink. The Long Island tea wasn't entirely harmless. It tasted of something alcoholic but nothing potent, and Laura was thirsty.

It didn't take her long to drain the tall glass. She felt a pleasant rush of warmth through her veins, a warmth that escalated into a feeling of heat. Despite the air-conditioning, the room began to seem a little too close, hot and over-crowded.

Laura stumbled over to the towering wall of windows. Leaning against them, she pressed the cool glass to her cheek. The ultramodern beach house with its vast ceiling and contemporary furnishings was not to her taste, but the view was magnificent. She gazed down to where the sun was setting on the horizon, spreading fiery fingers across the sea, the waves frothing over a shoreline that looked bright, new and untouched.

The sight was enough to make her forget how Chelsey's high heels tortured her feet and the dull pounding that had begun behind Laura's temples, making her feel a bit fuzzy. She experienced that familiar itch in her fingers, longing for her sketch pad.

A light, warm touch on her bare back caused Laura to stiffen. She spun around, almost fearing she was going to have Chad to fend off again. But it was Adam.

Laura sagged back, feeling glad to see him. Too glad. His presence was beginning to affect her like something between a warm blaze and jolt of electricity. And she wasn't sure that was good.

"So, did you survive running the gauntlet with my mother?" he asked with one of his slow, sexy smiles.

"Yes, thanks so much for coming to my rescue, Mr. Bond."

"I can't whisk you away in my gadget car all the time. I knew Lou would have no peace until she showed you off to all her friends. I think she's trying to put an end to the rumor that I'm going to shave my head and become a Buddhist monk."

An unexpected giggle escaped Laura. She eyed Adam through the thickness of her lashes, taking in the lean, flat plane of his hips, the hard, muscular wall of his chest, the totally masculine angles of his face. She had never seen a less likely candidate for monkhood or whatever it was called.

His smile became rueful. "I hope Lou didn't come on too strong. I should have warned you that she's in the market for more grandchildren, and I'm going to be thirty-five next September. I guess I'm making her a little desperate."

Laura shook her head. The movement seemed to make her dizzy, so she stopped. "Your mother is charming and the party is charming and the house is—"

"You're not going to say the house is charming."

"It's..." Laura raised her hand in a wildly expansive gesture. "It's big."

"I designed it to please Lou."

"It suits her. She's very modern."

"And what about Chelsey Stuart?" Adam leaned closer. His eyes looked rather hazy, or maybe it was only her own vision that was blurring. Laura rubbed her eyes to clear them.

"Oh, I'm not nearly so modern as you might think. I like old-fashioned things."

"Like miniskirts."

She regarded Adam through dreamy, half-closed eyes. "More like hoopskirts and crinolines. Memories of times when the world seemed a lot slower, more romantic."

Laura had a notion she was talking utter nonsense. But she was feeling incredibly mellow. Maybe it had something to do with the fact that she had the most attractive man in the room at her side and his attention seemed entirely focused on her.

And maybe it was something Chelsey had put in the tea. Laura blinked and turned back to stare out the window. Anything to keep from losing herself too deep in the gray mists of Adam's eyes. The sun had nearly set, the mysterious purple shadows of twilight darkening the shore.

"I didn't know stretches of beach this unspoiled existed anymore," she said.

"It's a private beach. No jet skis, no tourists with beach umbrellas. No planes flying overhead with banners saying 'Eat at Joe's.'" He was standing so close behind her, his voice rumbled pleasantly in her ear. She resisted an urge to sigh and nestle back against him. "Actually, that's the best thing about this place. We're pretty isolated here. The nearest neighbor is half a mile up the beach. You could even indulge your favorite pastime."

Laura angled a puzzled glance up at him.

"You're fond of sunbathing naked, aren't you?" he asked. "You must have been crushed when they closed that nudist colony up the coast."

His teasing no longer seemed to carry the same sarcastic bite to it. And Laura was able to shoot back, "Don't sneer unless you've tried it, Barnhart. All that—that sunshine and fresh air."

"I've got too much healthy respect for my—er—tender parts to expose them to sunburn."

"I wouldn't want you risking your tender parts, either," Laura said, then was a little stunned.

It was an outrageous remark and thoroughly Chelsey. And Laura had made it without blushing. Maybe she was getting better at this.

"I'd be inclined to be more daring in the moonlight," Adam murmured, his breath stirring her hair.

"But I don't have any buttons to tempt you with tonight."

"You could always help me with mine."

A shiver coursed through Laura. She was flirting with Adam and enjoying every minute of it, enjoying the heat in his gaze as it traveled over her bare shoulders, enjoying the rustling whisper of the red silk next to her skin. For the first time that evening, she was glad she had worn the blasted dress.

She nearly forgot that she and Adam were in a room crowded with other people until they were interrupted by a petite teenage girl. Her long baby-fine blond hair swayed about her shoulders as she came bobbing up to them.

"Hi," she said, flashing a grin, metallic with braces.

Adam seemed to ease away, reluctantly putting distance between himself and Laura. "Hi, yourself, brat. Chelsey, I don't think you've met my niece yet. This is Luke's sister, Jolene."

"Joey," the girl corrected, wrinkling her nose. "I've been dying to meet you, Chelsey. Do you really take pictures of naked men for *She* magazine?"

Laura winced. Bluntness seemed to run in the Barnhart family. "No, I don't have that particular job yet," she said. Or at least not that Chelsey had troubled to inform her.

"And what do you know about *She* magazine, young lady?" Adam growled.

"Oh, you're such a chauvinist, Uncle Adam," Joey said. "I'll bet you didn't care if Luke looked at naked pictures when he was my age."

"Yes, I did."

Joey turned long-suffering eyes on Laura. "He's so-o-o-o old-fashioned. Don't you think it would be fun taking photos of all those gorgeous hunks up close and personal?"

"Well, I—I..." Laura faltered, aware of Adam's expression of thunderous disapproval. "No, I don't think most women really enjoy looking at naked strangers."

"Speak for yourself, honey," one of the female guests piped up. She looked old enough to have been Laura's grandmother. Laura became uncomfortably aware that the conversation had captured the attention of half the room. Joey's voice was very penetrating.

Laura gulped and continued, "I think it's different for women than men. Women prefer looking at naked men who—whom they know."

Dozens of fascinated eyes seemed trained on her. Lou Barnhart's poker club was listening with avid interest. Laura had the sensation of sinking in deeper with every word she spoke.

"Men whom they know and—and care about," Laura concluded weakly.

"And what man do you care enough about to see naked, Miss Stuart?" The incorrigible Joey giggled. "Kevin Costner? Mel Gibson?"

"Well, I..." To Laura's horror, her gaze flew straight to Adam. It was as involuntary a reaction as breathing. As involuntary as the images that flitted through her mind. Adam, wet and naked on the beach, water dripping off the hairs matting his chest, the golden rays of the sun outlining the hard, lean contours of his—

The level of heat in the room suddenly became unbearable.

"Excuse me," Laura gasped, one hand fluttering to her throat. "I think I need a breath of air."

Avoiding Adam's eyes, she somehow managed to stumble from the room.

Five

She'd given him a look that had gone through him like a hot knife and then simply disappeared. But Adam was frustrated by his mother's guests in his efforts to follow Chelsey. Dr. Leaming cornered him and wanted to know the current price on Barnhart Shipping stocks. How the devil should Adam know? It was the first day he could remember that he hadn't once called in to the office to check up on business.

But there seemed to be no escaping the garrulous doctor. Adam fumed, torn between his desire to go after Chelsey and to give his pert niece a smack. Joey had upset Chelsey somehow with all her nonsense about naked men. And that was odd. Such a thing shouldn't have bothered a woman of Chelsey's uninhibited reputation.

But then there were a lot of things that shouldn't have upset Chelsey that did. Reporters, lurid notices in the press, holding her own in a roomful of strangers. The woman was as much a puzzle to Adam as when he'd first met her.

Shaking loose of the dentist, Adam was finally able to go in search of her. As soon as he figured out she wasn't in the house, it wasn't difficult to discover where she'd gone. All he had to do was follow the trail of discarded high heels.

He picked one up just outside the sliding doors leading out from the kitchen, and the other was at the end of the deck. Leaning against the rail, he peered down toward the backyard. None of the patio lights had been left on, except those in the pool itself. He spotted Chelsey seated at the edge of the deep end, dangling her toes in the water.

He could understand why she'd chosen to come out here. It was dark. It was quiet. And it was far too humid to tempt any of the guests to join her that far from the air-conditioning, one of those hot, steamy summer nights not even the breeze from the ocean could make comfortable.

Or maybe most of the steam was coming from him. Adam ran one finger along the inside of his collar. He could just make out Chelsey's curved silhouette by the reflection of the pool lights. Moonlight glimmered off her bare shoulders, her dress shifted up enough to expose a flash of white thigh.

Adam sucked in his breath and was tempted to go back in the house. He had resolved to keep his distance from Chelsey Stuart tonight. After that little jaunt down the coast with her in the sports car, he'd already been entertaining enough fantasies about Chelsey's long, graceful legs, how it would feel to cradle himself between those smooth, silken thighs. It had made for an interesting trip, in which Adam hadn't been sure which had been harder, the gearshift or himself.

He had only prolonged the agony by taking the longer way down Route 9, looping to the old seacoast road. But much as he hated to admit it, he had enjoyed the lady's company. She was intelligent, she was funny, she was easy to talk to. He hadn't wanted to like her and he knew he shouldn't trust her. The papers were still too full of rumors connecting her to Xavier Storm. But she had the most compellingly honest eyes he'd ever seen. One smile, one look from her was enough to send his heart doing flip-flops like a flounder caught in a net.

She made it damn difficult for him to remember that his purpose this weekend was to keep Luke out of female trouble, not to wade neck deep into it himself. With a regretful sigh, Adam half turned to go back into the house. But at that moment, Chelsey arched her neck, shaking her glorious fall of sable-dark hair down her back. It was a gesture at once both innocent and sensual. The lure she presented was as ageless as that first temptation in the Garden of Eden, and Adam felt as powerless as his namesake to resist it.

Tucking the shoes under his arm, he made his way off the deck, down to the patio. He saw her nylons dangling off the end of the umbrella table, the gossamer fabric shifting in the breeze like some enticing beacon.

She didn't glance up at his approach, just kept staring down at her toes, curling them in the water. He'd never thought much about feet being attractive before, but Chelsey's were beautiful. Small and dainty, with delicate, high arches. No wonder Victorian gents used to get turned on just by the sight of a shapely ankle.

She appeared subdued, her eyes soft and liquid as if she were lost in some haunting world of her own. Adam almost felt like an intruder in his own backyard, but he produced the shoes from beneath his arm.

"Lose something, Miss Stuart?"

Laura glanced up to find Adam towering over her, Chelsey's heels cupped in his outstretched hands. She wished he hadn't come. She didn't know what Chelsey had put in that tea, but Laura feared she was a little drunk, fast approaching the maudlin stage.

She feared even more that she had made a fool of herself back there at the party, flirting with Adam, spouting off her own prim philosophy about nudity, giving Adam a look of such raw hunger that no one could have failed to notice. Real sophisticated, Laura, she thought with a grimace. It would take far more than a red silk dress to turn dull Laura Stuart into a woman of Chelsey's daring and smooth wit.

Ducking her head, Laura mumbled. "You didn't have to find my shoes for me. Actually, I was hoping I'd never see those torture devices again."

"Consider them gone." Adam strode over in the direction of the gas grill. Startled, Laura watched him toss Chelsey's expensive Italian shoes into a small trash bin. Chelsey would go ballistic. The thought gave Laura a shameful twinge of satisfaction. So far, she thought, the cost of this little adventure had all been set down to her account.

But her fleeting smile vanished as Adam returned and pulled up a deck chair. "Mind if I join you?" he asked.

Did she? Yes—she wanted him to go away. Yet even more strongly, she wanted him to stay. It dismayed her to realize she was starting to want many things from Adam. Like for him to be attracted to her as Laura, not Laura masquerading as Chelsey.

She turned back to swirling her feet through the water, watching the lights shimmer at the bottom of the pool.

"You'd better go," she said. "You're too dangerous in the moonlight, Barnhart."

"So are you." He laughed softly and sat down anyway.

"Oh, yeah, I'm a real threat to the male sex," Laura muttered. One of the sleeves of Chelsey's dress slipped too low, and Laura hiked it back up again. As soon as this masquerade was over, no more lady in red, she thought. She would be back to—to being beige again. That was another miserable effect of this impersonation. She had never expected to be left with such sharp dissatisfaction regarding her own life.

The silence stretched out, the only sound the distant music and laughter filtering down from the house. Laura was keenly aware of Adam sitting behind her in the dark. She could almost feel the weight of his stare. Not one of his heated looks. She would have been more comfortable with that. He seemed to be studying her like some puzzle that he sought to unravel. The puzzle would be solved for him as soon as she could tell him who she really was. Chelsey Stuart was the enigma, Laura thought wryly. Laura Stuart was about as mysterious as—as a peanut-butter-and-jelly sandwich.

"You ought to scoot back a little," he said at last. "You're going to fall in."

"Are those the kinds of warnings you give your niece and nephew, Uncle Adam?"

"No, Luke and Joey are both good swimmers."

"Well, so is Chelsey Stuart. She could have been an Olympic contender."

"In a cocktail dress?"

In any kind of dress, Laura reflected, where she herself feared she would sink like a rock, even wearing a life vest. Laura had never learned to swim. "Not with your asthma," her mother had always said. It would be far too great a risk.

But she had outgrown all that. Laura wondered why she still continued to live her life as if she were one of those china figurines encased in glass. In defiance of Adam's warning, of her own common sense, she scooted closer to the edge, the red silk dress flowing out around her.

"Kind of a waste, isn't it?" she asked. "Having a pool with the ocean so near?"

Adam got to his feet and paced off a few restless steps. "I had the pool put in mostly for Joey. She's not crazy about the ocean. Too many little slimy things oozing between her toes, she says."

"And you designed the house to please your mother. Tell me something, Adam. Do you ever do anything just to please you?"

The question seemed to surprise him. His lips quirked in an odd half smile. "Yes, I rescued a leggy brunette from a hoard of ravenous reporters."

"You didn't seem to enjoy it much at the time," Laura reminded him.

He rubbed his chin. "Looking back on it, it was kind of fun. 'Uncle Adam' doesn't have adventures very often. He has to take them where he can find them."

It was strange to hear him saying such a thing, such a close echo of her own feelings. A man who looked like he did ought to lead a very exciting life, his hard-edged features replete with a kind of raw sensuality. From the beginning, she'd thought Adam Barnhart could be anything he wanted to be, from a hard-boiled detective to a CIA operative.

But he wasn't. He was the president of his family's ship company. He was Uncle Adam.

The thought slipped out before she could stop it. "You look too young to be anyone's uncle."

"I feel like I've aged a great deal lately." He hunkered down beside her, trailing his hand in the water. The pool lights illuminated his profile, the lines that crinkled by his eyes when he smiled and made him sexy as hell. But they were lines that also seemed too deep for a man who hadn't yet seen his thirty-fifth birthday.

"How long has it been since your older brother—" Laura blurted out. "Well, ah, I mean, since he..."

The hand Adam had in the water went still. "Jack was killed in a plane crash when Luke was ten, Joey about five.

They had lost their mother to cancer two years before that. It was hard on them."

Hard on Adam, too, although Laura doubted he would ever admit such a thing. A dull, empty look crept into his eyes. He was quick to straighten, taking his face back into the shadows.

"So how long have you been their guardian?" Laura persisted.

"About twelve years."

"Twelve years! Why, you must have... have been—"

"Not much older than Luke is now," he finished flatly.

"What a terrifying responsibility it must have been for you."

"I managed." Adam shrugged, as ever uncomfortable with any expression of sympathy. He had received too many condolences after his brother's death. Everyone had said "how sad," "how tragic" and "how lucky the children are to have you." But no one had ever perceived what Laura did, how terrified he'd been to fill Jack's shoes, how scared he still was sometimes.

He cleared his throat and said gruffly, "It was easier when the kids were younger, especially Luke. All I used to worry about was him breaking his arm instead of..."

"His heart?" she filled in. "You don't have to worry about that, Adam, at least not with my sister." She hesitated, seeming to choose her words with care. "L.C. tends to build walls around herself. She makes a lot of friends, though she doesn't often give her love. But when she does, it's forever."

"Actually, it wasn't broken hearts I was worried about, so much as broken dreams. They're just as hard to replace."

"And what dreams have you let slip away, Adam Barnhart?"

Even in the semidarkness, Laura's remarkable green gold eyes were far too penetrating.

"I was talking about Luke," Adam said. "I don't know whether L.C. has told you, but he's musically gifted. He's completed four years at the Jersey Symphonic Conservatory and has been accepted for postgrad work at Juilliard. I expect to see him playing piano at Carnegie Hall someday—unless he gets sidetracked."

"No, L.C. wouldn't do that. She understands what it means to have dreams, a special talent that means more than anything to you, that you just have to share with the world or—or burst."

Laura's voice had become far too passionate. She realized that and was suddenly unsure if she was speaking for Chelsey or herself.

"I just wish you could give L.C. a chance, Adam," she said.

"Maybe I could." Something in his tone made her look up. He had gone still, his hands in his pockets. His head tilted slightly to one side, he studied her, an odd expression on his face.

"Why don't you tell me about Laura Caroline Stuart," he suggested quietly.

"Well..." Laura moistened her lips. "She and I were very close when we were children. Then Laura—L.C.—got pneumonia which developed into asthma. After that, everything changed."

"Changed? How?"

It felt peculiar to be talking about herself in this third-person way. Laura squirmed, but continued, "My parents started tiptoeing around her, always afraid they were going to lose her. She learned to live her life from the living-room sofa, watching the world through our big front picture window.

"That's why she started drawing. It was her only way of bringing the world to her that seemed safe." Laura paused and added somewhat bitterly. "It was the one thing she could do that didn't get everyone all upset."

She sighed. "Her illness was hard on my family. My parents eventually got divorced and I guess that's when Chels—when I started running a bit wild."

"And you blame Laura for all that?"

"I don't know," Laura said sadly. "No, I suppose not. It wasn't her fault she was sick, and she's better now. She's put all that behind her."

"Has she?"

Adam's soft question discomfited her somehow. Laura had an uneasy feeling she had been talking too much. Leaning on her hands, she started to lift her legs out of the pool. But her right palm slipped. For a moment she teetered precariously. Her stomach gave a sickening lurch of fear as she lost her balance and fell in.

Even then she could have grabbed for the side, but as the tepid water closed over her head, blinding her, cutting off her air, Laura panicked. She thrashed about wildly, her dress tangled about her thighs.

Her awkward movements propelled her upward enough to break the surface. She gulped in a lungful of air, only to sink again. It was the worst of all her childhood nightmares, not being able to breathe.

She struggled, flailed, took in pool water, felt it burn her throat. She became aware of movement beside her, struck up against something. Adam's arms reached out to encircle her, lift her up to the surface. In her blind panic, she fought him, dragging them both back down.

But Adam got a firm hold around her neck and hauled her to the side of the pool. With one strong, fluid motion, he hoisted her out.

Laura collapsed, choking and sputtering, taking in great, painful gasps of air. As her terror subsided, she realized she couldn't have been in the water more than a few seconds, but her heart still raced wildly.

She became conscious that Adam sprawled beside her, panting. He looked as shaken as she was. Shoving his wet hair back from his eyes, he glared at her.

"Damn it. I warned you. Stay back from the edge."

She didn't need him reminding her how stupid she'd been. She opened her mouth to tell him so, but her teeth started chattering. Not from the cold, but a belated reaction to her recent terror.

"Come here," he said. Struggling to a sitting position, he hauled her into his arms. He cradled her head against his chest, rocking her slowly back and forth. "It's all right."

His shirt was soaked, but his skin pulsed warm and soothing beneath the wet layer of fabric. Laura felt her heartbeat slow to a more normal rhythm, Adam's strong arms seeming like a bastion against anything that could go bump in the night. He had this comforting routine down well. The way he rocked her suggested years of practice. Laura could only wonder when she'd first met him, how had she ever imagined him to be such a hard, unfeeling man.

He stroked his hand through her wet hair, smoothing out the tangles. "What the hell happened? I thought you could swim."

Laura stiffened, easing herself out of his embrace. "I—I got a cramp in my leg."

"Which one?"

Laura glanced down at her exposed limbs. The right one seemed as good as any to blame it on. She pointed to her calf. "R-right there."

He eased his fingers around her leg. Carefully, firmly he began to knead the muscle beneath her skin. "I can't feel anything," he said with a puzzled frown. "Usually when a muscle cramps, it goes hard as a rock."

"It's a little better now."

Chelsey had always been good at faking injuries. The girl had gotten herself out of more gym-class calisthenics that way. Laura had never even attempted such a thing until now. She tensed her muscle for Adam's benefit. It wasn't too difficult, not with the warm feel of his hands on her bare leg.

She shivered, yet she wasn't cold. If anything, the night was far too warm. She tried to remember that Adam working his hands up and down her calf was for medicinal purposes only. But his touch, so strong, so intimate against her flesh, sent rivers of heat coursing through her.

She noted with dismay how her wet dress clung to her, revealing the swell of her breasts, the curve of her thighs. She could tell the exact moment when awareness struck Adam, too.

His fingers hesitated, becoming less firm, more caressing. The shirt plastered to the hard contours of his chest was almost transparent, his hair slick against his brow, drops of pool water beading along his jaw, near the sensual curve of his mouth.

His gaze became darker, his fingers stroking out a rhythm that evoked tingling sensations all along her skin. Laura was embarrassed to note her nipples standing out taut and firm, outlined to perfection beneath the wet red silk.

She gulped and leaned forward, catching Adam's wrist. "It's fine now."

"You sure?" His fingers lingered at the sensitive hollow behind her knee, the touch warm and suggestive.

"I—I guess so."

He drew closer, so that his face was only inches from her own. "I never took care of a half-drowned woman before," he said huskily. "Isn't there something else I should do?"

She stared into the dark mists of his gray eyes and felt as if she were drowning all over again. She moistened her lips. "Well, I—I think it's customary to give mouth-to-mouth."

"Like this?"

His lips covered hers, their warm, rough texture lightly coaxing hers apart. A faint murmur escaped Laura, whether of protest or agreement she wasn't sure, until Adam cupped his hand behind her neck, his mouth becoming more demanding.

Laura's hands moved up his shoulders of their own volition. She wrapped her arms around him. Begging him to deepen the kiss, she let her mouth go soft and pliant, inviting him to tease, to taste, to fill her with heat.

As one, they eased back down, stretched out side by side. His mouth still imprisoning hers, Adam urged her closer, pressing one hand against her bottom, entwining her legs with his. His touch was like fire, the soaked silk so scant a barrier she might as well have been naked.

She could feel the hard throb of his own desire as he kissed her, the passion mounting between them. Passion as wild and tender as the night. Passion as strong and thundering as the seas.

His hand found her breast, even through the slick, wet fabric, branding her with the heat of his palm, caressing, stroking until her nipple ached with a pleasure that was almost unbearable.

With a soft moan, Laura arched back, offering up the sensitive hollow of her throat to his feverish kiss. The sweet taste of her, the creamy texture of her skin stirred Adam to the point of madness.

With her damp hair splayed about her bare white shoulders, her soft pink lips parted in surrender, she reminded Adam of erotic visions he'd entertained of mermaids, seductive sirens cast upon the shore, during lonely walks by the sea.

He wanted her, wanted her so much he was fairly shaken with the need. He could almost believe she did have him bewitched, and as his mouth sought hers again he was in no hurry to break the spell.

But the enchantment shattered soon enough when the patio lamps suddenly flicked on, flooding the backyard like searchlights. With a curse, Adam wrenched himself away from Chelsey. He bolted to his feet, using his body to shield her as she struggled to right her dress.

He felt as mortified as a teenage boy caught with his pants down. He must have been out of his mind, practically making love to Chelsey Stuart in full view of the house, where anyone might be likely to come out and find them.

That anyone turned out to be Joey. She crept out on the deck, peering over the rail. "Uncle Adam?"

Those two words had never filled him with such dread. He'd never felt less like being Uncle Adam than he did at this moment, his body still aching with frustrated desire. He extended a hand to Chelsey, to help her to her feet, hardly daring to look at her, her face flushed, her lips still soft and tempting from his kiss.

Adam called out tersely, "Go back in the house, Joey. I'll be there in a minute."

But she was already bouncing down the deck steps.

"Hell!" Adam muttered, bracing for a barrage of giggling teenage-girl curiosity. He silently damned himself for his own irresponsible behavior.

It was some small relief to realize Joey could not have seen much. Otherwise her eyes would not have gone so wide as she took in his and Chelsey's bedraggled appearance.

"Holy smokes! What happened to you two?"

"I—I accidently fell in," Chelsey spoke up. "Your uncle came to my rescue."

"With your clothes on? All right!" Joey grinned. "It looks like fun."

The little idiot would have been in the pool in another minute if Adam hadn't caught her by the arm and hauled her back.

"Why don't you make yourself useful, Jolene? Go back to the house and get us some towels."

"Okay." She shrugged. "I only came out to see what you and Chelsey were doing out here in the dark, anyway." She chuckled and then added. "You missed Luke's big announcement."

"Shut up, Joey." Luke's voice boomed down from the deck.

Adam stifled a groan. Not his nephew, too. Now all he needed was his mother out here. And Lou wondered why Adam never seemed to find a spare moment to get himself engaged.

Luke bounded down into the yard, glaring at his younger sister. "Aren't you a little old to go tattling to Uncle Adam?"

"I wouldn't have to, if you had the guts to tell him yourself," Joey shot back.

"Tell me what?" Adam asked.

"Why don't you mind your own business, Jolene?" Luke asked.

"Why don't you make me, nerd?"

Adam pinched the bridge of his nose, feeling his temper start to fray. For two people who were constantly assuring him what adults they were, Jolene and Luke sounded like two bickering kids again. And Adam, aware of Chelsey's silent presence, didn't feel up to playing mediator tonight.

He snapped out a sharp command, ordering Jolene back to the house. She listened to him for once, but the way she kept lingering, looking back as if she expected some explosion, filled Adam with foreboding.

As soon as the door banged shut behind her, Adam turned to Luke. The look on his nephew's face wasn't reassuring. The jut of his jaw was defiant, but Luke didn't seem able to meet Adam's eyes.

"So what was the big announcement I wasn't meant to hear?" Adam asked.

"You were meant to hear it. You just weren't there." Luke kicked his toe at the top of the ladder that stretched down into the pool. "I decided I'm not going back to school next fall."

Oh, Lord, Laura thought, sucking in her breath. She took one look at the grim expression settling over Adam's features and wished she were safe back in the house with Jolene.

"Excuse me," she murmured and tried to slip past Adam. But his hand settled over her wrist in an iron grip.

"Oh, no, stay where you are, Chelsey." His dark eyes seemed to stab at her with accusation. "I take it this is no big secret from anyone but me, Luke?"

Luke shrugged. "No big secret. No big deal, either. I'm just tired of school, that's all."

"Tired of it? You've been give a chance to continue studying your music at one of the most prestigious schools in the country and you're *tired* of it. Tell me. When did this brilliant revelation come over you?"

Laura could see Adam's sarcasm lash the sensitive young man like a whip. She understood the fear, the concern that motivated Adam's anger, but she wished she could have made him moderate his tone.

"It's only become real clear to me lately," Luke said.

"In other words, since you met L.C. Stuart."

"L.C. has nothing to do with this. She's been a good friend to me, that's all."

"And does your good friend know I control your trust fund until you're twenty-five?"

Laura's own protest at this insinuation was cut off by Luke's outraged cry. "To hell with the trust fund! It doesn't interest me or L.C. We're planning to take a trip cross-country until I get my head together, figure out what I want to do. L.C. thinks I could get some pretty good gigs as a saxophone player."

Oh, Chelsey, Laura thought with a groan. What kind of mischief have you stirred up now? And why, as usual, aren't you here to deal with it?

Adam was all but crushing Laura's wrist. She managed to wrench free. He paced off a few agitated steps, his face almost white. She could tell he was making a herculean effort to control his temper.

He came to a dead halt and snapped out a single word. "No."

"What do you mean?" Luke asked.

"I mean this is as far as this stupidity is going to go. I don't want to hear any more about it. You were perfectly content until you mixed up with that—"

"No, I wasn't, Adam. I tried to tell you that lots of times. But you just never listen. I'm capable of making my own decisions now. I'm not a kid anymore."

"Then stop acting like one."

Luke shook his head bitterly. "I told L.C. how it would be. I knew you'd react like this." Pivoting on his heel, he stalked back toward the house.

"This discussion is not over, Luke," Adam shouted after him.

"As far as I'm concerned, it is." Luke vaulted up onto the deck. The sound of the door slamming behind him seemed to echo through the night.

Adam immediately started to charge after him. Laura knew she had no right to interfere, but she couldn't seem to help herself.

She caught Adam by the arm. "Adam, wait."

The fury in his eyes struck her with as much force as an actual blow. But Laura stood her ground.

"Don't go after Luke now," she pleaded. "It would be better if you waited, until you are both calmer."

He shook her off. "I don't need any more tips from you on how to handle my nephew. I've already had quite enough of your advice." Adam mimicked her words in an angry tone. "Give my sister a chance, Adam. L.C. understands about dreams. She wouldn't do anything to stand in Luke's way."

Laura winced. "I—I don't quite know what's happened here. But at least I am open-minded enough to wait before I pass judgment on anybody."

"I think you know perfectly well what's been going on. It wouldn't surprise me if you and your sister had this whole thing planned out all along. It's real convenient that I just happened to be out here with you when Luke made his little announcement. What were you supposed to do, Chelsey? Distract me? You did a damn good job of it."

Hot color flooded Laura's cheeks at the unreasonableness, the total unfairness of Adam's accusation. She wanted to remind him in no uncertain terms that it had been his own idea to follow her out to the pool.

But as usual when she got angry she felt her throat closing up, reducing her thoughts to a state of furious incoherency.

"Oh, yes, Mr. Barnhart," she managed to choke out. "I—I almost drowned myself just to—to keep you occupied."

"Are you going to tell me that leg cramp bit wasn't phony?"

Laura opened her mouth and closed it again. It only frustrated her more that she couldn't deny his words. Or explain herself without revealing the full extent of her deception.

"I had you and your sister pretty well pegged as trouble from the beginning," Adam said bitterly. "I don't know how I came to lose sight of that fact."

"And I don't know how I ever came to change my mind about you. You're just what I thought you were. An arrogant, pompous, opinionated..." Laura paused, struggling for a name bad enough to call him.

"Idiot," Adam supplied. "I was an idiot to have forgotten what I know about you. I was almost falling for you, for that whole big-eyed, sympathetic routine. If Joey hadn't come out when she did, I probably would have ended up just another notch on Chelsey Stuart's lipstick case. At least it's good to know where I stand again."

"You have no idea where you're standing, Barnhart," Laura ground out.

At the edge of the pool. And Laura took full advantage of that fact. Bringing her fists down hard on Adam's chest, she gave him a mighty shove.

He teetered on the edge and went flying backward.

There was a loud splash, followed by the sound of Adam's sputtered curse. But Laura was already storming her way back to the house.

Six

The morning light barely peeked through the blinds. But Laura gave the cord a vicious tug, flooding the bedroom with sunshine. Chelsey groaned and buried her head beneath the pillow of her twin bed, but Laura had not an ounce of sympathy for her. She'd not passed such a sterling night herself.

She didn't know exactly when Chelsey had finally tiptoed into the bedroom they shared at the beach house. Laura only knew that there had been another grim confrontation between Luke and Adam. She could hear the upraised voices even from her own room where she'd been changing into dry clothes. After that, Chelsey and Luke had disappeared somewhere down the beach.

Chelsey could not have returned until after two. Laura had been up herself until then, feeling irritated with the whole lot of them—Luke, Chelsey, Adam. Mostly Adam.

She had vented some of her frustrations in the usual way. Digging out the sketchbook she always traveled with, she had proceeded to etch out a new character for her Fur Toes series, a stern rabbit with long, arrogant whiskers and an overbearing expression. She had scrawled the caption beneath the drawing with grim satisfaction, *Uncle Carrots.*

It had always helped before, turning people who angered or upset her into ink strokes on the page. She had transformed her ex-fiancé, Tom, into a nearsighted bumblebee who was always flying into flowers and never recognizing what they were. But somehow reducing Adam to sketch form did nothing to soothe her lacerated feelings.

It appalled her to think of how she'd knocked him into the pool. She wasn't a woman given to violence. But the things he'd said, the harsh accusations he'd flung out against her, against Chelsey. The man was so blasted unreasonable he wouldn't stop to listen to any explanations. Laura shuddered to think what Adam would be like when he learned the truth of what was really going on.

Maybe the return to hostility between them had been a good thing. It gave Laura a chance to draw back from other feelings that had pulsed between her and Adam, emotions that had rocketed her along at the speed of light, a speed she wasn't prepared to handle. She'd always been more the plodding horse-and-buggy type.

How far would things have gone between Adam and her if Joey hadn't interrupted them? Would Laura have surrendered to his heated caress right there on the pavement by the pool, made wild, passionate love with a man she hardly knew? But that was part of the trouble. When she was in his arms, she kept sensing through every fiber of her being that she did know him, from all his stubborn flaws to all the magnificent tenderness and caring the man was capable of.

But that didn't matter. Because he didn't know her. The bitter words he'd flung out kept coming back to haunt her.

I was almost falling for you. But it wasn't Laura he was falling for. It was Chelsey. Or whoever this creation was that

Laura had concocted, this wanton female who liked hot red dresses and Adam's even hotter kisses. Who knocked men into swimming pools when they annoyed her.

If this masquerade went on any longer, Laura wasn't sure she would know herself anymore. Time to get back to Bennington Falls, where life was slow but sane. Time to get back to being beige again.

While Chelsey remained tunneled beneath the covers, Laura hauled her suitcase up on her own bed. She began yanking clothes out of the bureau drawers where Chelsey had stuffed them. Laura's own demure, safe ladylike children's author clothes.

She made no effort to be silent. She opened and slammed drawers with a vengeance until Chelsey emerged from beneath her pillow. She blinked owlishly at Laura and stretched, only to stop in mid-yawn when she saw the suitcase.

"What are you doing, Laura?"

"It's called packing."

Chelsey staggered out of bed, groping for a flimsy robe to throw over her T-shirt and skimpy lace panties. Shaking her head as if to clear away the last vestiges of sleep, she moaned, "Come on, Laura. Don't do anything hasty."

Laura compressed her lips and scooped up a handful of her bras and underpants from the drawer. Chelsey was momentarily distracted.

"Geez, you still wear the same kind of white cotton briefs Aunt Gussie used to send us for Christmas."

"Leave my underwear out of this," Laura said, flinging the garments into the suitcase. "I waited up half the night for you, Chelsey, so we could talk about this mess we're in. I have a splitting headache. What did you put in that drink you gave me, anyway?"

"A little of this and a little of that. Some rum, vodka and whiskey." Chelsey gave an airy shrug. "I guess you must be upset about that fight between Luke and Adam last night, huh?''

''Good guess.'' Laura paused in the act of going for her blow dryer to glare at her sister. ''I went way out on a limb for you, Chelsey, and you sawed it off behind me. I almost had Adam convinced he could trust you not to interfere with Luke's dream of being a concert pianist.''

''Luke's dream or the one Adam thinks he should have? Adam has that poor boy so confused, he thinks it's his duty to become the next—the next Stradivarius.''

''A Stradivarius is a violin,'' Laura stated.

''Whatever it is, Luke doesn't want to be it. He's not sure what he wants.''

''And running off with you is supposed to help? You've never known what you wanted to do with your life, either.''

''Unlike you,'' Chelsey said bitterly. ''Sensible, responsible Laura. Everything's always so clear to you. Right and wrong. Black and white.''

Laura felt the argument between Chelsey and her drifting into the familiar, painful lines. She turned to resume her packing. Chelsey flounced to the window and stood with her arms folded, staring out.

''I haven't been acting too sensible lately,'' Laura said. ''I should never have agreed to this crazy masquerade. It's only made everything worse.''

''It was my fault. I dragged you into it.''

''But as the older sister—''

''Am I going to have to hear about those two minutes for the rest of my life?'' Chelsey spun about to face Laura. ''I realize I'm probably not the best influence on Luke. But damn it, Laura, I love him. This classical-musician thing is just not right for him. I can feel it. You've got to trust my instincts on this one, not Adam's.''

Laura stirred uneasily, remembering. It had been Chelsey who had goaded Laura into throwing over her opportunity for a nice, secure job at the library to risk everything, turning what Laura had feared could only be a charming hobby into a successful writing career. She'd never really thanked her sister for that. It was remarkable and kind of sad, Chelsey's knack for prodding others to realize their dreams. Chelsey, who never seemed able to find one of her own.

"So what do you think Luke ought to do?" Laura asked.

"I don't know yet. But I do know he's never going to have a chance to find himself, not while he's stuck under Adam's thumb."

"Adam only acts that way because he cares," Laura snapped, surprised to find herself defending the man.

"Adam's caring is smothering Luke, and you ought to know what that feels like."

"Maybe I do, but your meddling isn't helping. All you've done is to get Luke and Adam at each other's throats. Luke's going to go off with you, leaving a big rift between him and Adam. Adam seems like a hard case, but beneath his tough act I know it's going to hurt him, and I care too much about him to. . ."

Laura saw Chelsey's eyes go wide. Laura paused, stunned herself by what she'd been about to say.

"You care too much about Adam?" Chelsey echoed incredulously. "A guy you met two days ago? This from the Laura Stuart who took two years to make up her mind to get engaged to that ophthalmologist."

"I probably should've taken longer," Laura said. Or known much sooner that she hadn't been in love with Tom Carruthers. Was it possible she had been with Tom for two years and not once had he been able to arouse her desire, to touch her heart the way Adam seemed able to do with a single glance?

But to be in love with Adam Barnhart after only two days? The thought was frightening. She was becoming as wild and impulsive with her emotions as Chelsey.

Chelsey shifted her bare feet awkwardly against the carpet. "I'm sorry, hon. I didn't mean to rake over old coals."

"It's all right. Tom didn't break my heart. Catching him cheating on me hurt my pride more than anything else. Left me feeling a little lost. He was so nice and safe." Laura winced over the word. "Always a guaranteed dinner date for Saturday night, a warm bed to go to on a Wednesday afternoon."

"You had sex with the ophthalmologist?"

Laura felt herself color a little. "Well, we did go together for two years."

"I always assumed you were the last of the great American virgins."

"No, I took care of that when I was seventeen." Laura's lips quirked into a rueful smile. "One of my rare flings with rebellion. Totally stupid, totally awkward and adolescent. I made out with Ed Barnes in the back of his dad's pickup. He had asthma, too. I had to let him share my inhaler."

Laura expected that Chelsey would laugh, especially after her own string of highly exciting, highly romantic sexual escapades. But Chelsey just stood staring at Laura, the look in her eyes strange, even a little wistful.

It was hard to remember sometimes, Laura thought, that she and Chelsey were identical twins, sisters who should have been closer, known each other better, shared each other's every secret. She and Chelsey really had become like strangers.

Laura turned and closed the latch on her suitcase. The movement seemed to snap Chelsey out of her trance. "Oh, God, I'm sorry, Laura," she said. "I never imagined there could be anything going on between you and Adam."

"There isn't. He thinks I'm you, remember?"

Chelsey dragged her hand back through her disordered brown hair and groaned. "What a major disaster I've created this time."

Laura was not about to disagree with her.

Chelsey placed her hand atop Laura's on the suitcase. "Don't go, Laura. I'll get everything straightened out. I swear it."

When Laura started to shake her hand away, Chelsey rushed on, "Luke and I are driving up to Hammonton today to visit some of his second cousins. Considering the tension between him and Adam, it seems better not to hang around here. I'll—I'll use the time to talk to Luke. I still think he's right not to go back to school, but I'll convince him to be a little more patient with Adam's concern."

"And is that all you're going to talk to Luke about?"

"No." Chelsey vented a deep sigh. "I'll tell him who I really am. But it's not going to be easy, confessing to the man you care about that you've been lying through your teeth ever since you first met him."

"Tell me about it," Laura muttered.

Chelsey wrapped her arm about Laura's shoulders. "Oh, hon, please just try to hold out a little longer. If you betray me to Adam first, he'll go straight to Luke, and I may never have a chance to make Luke understand. This is so important to me."

Laura compressed her lips, trying to resist that pleading tone, but she could already feel her grip upon the suitcase weakening. "You swear to me that by tonight you will have told Luke everything?"

"I swear."

"All right. I'll give you twelve more hours." Laura consulted her watch. "Until nine o'clock tonight, and that's all."

Chelsey enveloped her in a fierce hug. "You're the best, kiddo."

"But what am I supposed to do in the meantime? I don't think I'm up to continuing this performance for the rest of the Barnhart family."

Especially Adam.

"Luke and I can drop you off at Belle's Point," Chelsey said. "You can go shopping. I'll bet there's some musty, old bookstore you can poke around in, and you can catch the local bus back up this way anytime you get tired." Chelsey cast her one final, anxious glance. "You really will wait until nine o'clock before telling Adam, won't you, Laura? No matter what happens, you'll remember your promise."

"Yes, I'll remember," Laura said glumly. The way matters stood between her and Adam at the moment, Laura doubted the truth was going to make any difference to him, one way or the other.

Laura finished with the attractions to be found in Belle's Point in about an hour. She almost felt that going there had been a mistake. She hadn't even seen Adam that morning. He had disappeared before breakfast. Louise Barnhart and Joey had likewise pursued occupations of their own. There was no one left back at the beach house.

No one except Chad Leaming, Laura reminded herself with a grimace. He'd been hired by the Barnharts to clean their pool. Laura had had no desire to be left alone with *him*. Even wandering the streets of Belle's Point seemed preferable.

There was a used-book shop and several antique stores that should have lured her into browsing, but she didn't seem to be in the mood. The only shop where Laura ended up making a purchase was a lady's boutique specializing in intimate apparel.

It was unexpected finding such a store in a little town like Belle's Point, and it made Laura wonder what the local fishermen's wives were up to at night. She didn't know what possessed her to patronize the place. Maybe it was the crack Chelsey had made about Laura's underwear...

She bought half a dozen pairs of lacy satin bikini pants and slunk out of the store, her merchandise stuffed in a pink plastic bag with the boutique's logo, Gertie's Garters, emblazoned on it. Laura would have preferred plain brown wrapping. She felt as conspicuous as if she'd been buying aphrodisiacs.

It was foolish. Who'd ever see the things besides herself, anyway, and it wasn't as though the wisps of satin exactly went well with flannel nightgowns and woolly bathrobes.

Tucking the bag beneath her arm, Laura consulted her watch. It wasn't even noon. Now what? She didn't see how she was going to kill the rest of the day here. The salesclerk at Gertie's Garters had mentioned something about a historic mansion worth looking at.

In sheer desperation Laura followed the woman's directions, heading down a side street that eventually wound back by the harbor. Beyond a wrought-iron fence, set across an expanse of green lawn, stood a majestic-looking house facing the bay.

Laura perked up a little at the sight of the stately Victorian with its whimsical gables, turrets and inviting veranda. This was more her notion of a seaside home than Louise Barnhart's ultramodern beach house. But the mansion had been allowed to lapse into a state of disrepair, paint peeling, much of the elaborate gingerbread trim chipped away. It reminded Laura of some faded, aging beauty staring out over the harbor, waiting for her man to return from the sea.

Laura approached as far as the front walkway, then hesitated. The house appeared too deserted to be open to the public, but Laura could hear an incessant hammering. She followed the sound around the side of the veranda and saw a broad-shouldered carpenter perched on a ladder, attempting to repair some rotted wood in the siding.

A carpenter who looked like Adam! Laura froze and blinked, wondering if the sun was playing tricks on her eyes. Her gaze skimmed over the familiar hard, tanned profile, the sweep of ash gold hair resting crisply against his collar.

It was definitely Adam, looking much drier than when she'd last seen him. And a lot more casual, too, wearing faded denims that hugged the taut contours of his thighs and a soft chambray shirt rolled up to expose the powerful sinews of his forearms.

He was too intent upon his hammering to look around. Laura's first instinct was to creep quietly away again, although she was burning with curiosity to know why the executive of a shipping company was moonlighting as a handyman. But she felt like an actress caught out of costume.

She'd opted to wear her own clothes today, comfortable jeans made feminine by a camisole-style top of white eyelet. She'd done her hair in a very demure, very Laura-like french braid. But before Laura could make up her mind what to do, Adam chanced to look up from his task.

Surprise flared in his eyes and he drove the hammer down on his thumb instead of the nail. Laura winced for him as he shook out his injured hand with a string of soft curses. Then he glowered at her, his heavy brows drawing together.

"Where the hell did you come from?" he snapped.

It was hardly the most auspicious beginning for mending fences between them. But Laura came forward. "I'm sorry," she said. "I didn't mean to startle you."

Shifting her bag beneath her arm, she stopped by the base of the ladder, angling her face up toward his. His eyes roved over her, a flicker of uncertainty crossing his features.

"Chelsey?"

Laura hesitated over her reply. But she was still bound by her promise to her sister, and the hostility she detected in

Adam's voice didn't make this seem like the ideal time for any confessions.

"Yes, of course it's me," she said. She didn't want him to think for a moment she'd followed him here, especially after the things he'd said to her last night. So she rushed to explain to him how she came to be in town.

"And there was no one left at the house but Chad Leaming."

"My mother hires him to do odd jobs," Adam said. "He cracked up his motorcycle and his parents refused to buy him another one. He's desperate for some cash, so Lou felt she ought to encourage the kid to earn it for a change."

"Chad makes me very uncomfortable. I'm not sure I trust him."

"Yeah, well, there are probably many people who shouldn't be trusted." Adam went back to his hammering. The coldness in his tone washed over her like an ice bath.

She shifted her feet, feeling awkward and a little resentful. Apparently, she was prepared to be more generous about forgetting the heated words they had exchanged last night than he was.

"So where did Lou and Joey go?" he demanded.

"Your mother drove Joey over to a friend's. She's going on some kind of overnight trip."

"Overnight! What kind of overnight?"

"I'm not sure. Something to do with Senior Scouts, I guess."

"I'm supposed to be the girl's guardian. Why the hell doesn't anybody ever tell me about these things?" He paused, giving Laura a dark look, as if she were somehow responsible for this as well.

"If you hurry, you can still have the organization checked out by the FBI," Laura said curtly. Spinning on her heel, she started to stalk away.

But she hadn't covered more than a few feet when she heard Adam say, "Chelsey . . . wait!"

She came around to face him, her bearing stiff, one hand placed on her hip. Adam had descended the ladder. He stared at her for a moment, working his jaw. The words seemed to cost him great effort, but he got them out. "I'm sorry. About how I acted just now. And last night, too. I can be a real bastard sometimes."

"Only sometimes?"

He sighed. "It's my damned temper. I say things I don't mean."

It was hard to resist the genuine regret in his voice, harder still when Laura noticed the haggard lines creasing his face. Adam obviously had not slept much last night, either.

"You were right," he said gruffly. "I should have left Luke alone until I cooled down. We had a pretty big blowup."

"I know. I couldn't help hearing."

Adam flinched. "I imagine they heard us all the way to Cape May. And now Luke's gone off with your sister. Maybe he won't be back."

"Yes, he will."

"He said . . ." Adam swallowed. "He said I was messing up his life."

"I'm sure he didn't mean it."

"He's probably right. I sat up half the night thinking about some of things you said, about me being overbearing, not letting Luke make his own decisions. But all I was ever trying to do—" Adam raked his hand back through his hair, his voice rife with sorrow and frustration. "Damn it, I only wanted what I thought was best for him."

"Sometimes what's best is just letting go," Laura said gently.

"I've never been good at letting anything go—except my temper."

"It's all right to lose your temper occasionally," Laura said, finding herself eager to reassure him, to do anything to drive back the shadows from his eyes. "I tend to hold things inside way too much."

That coaxed an unexpected laugh from him. Laura thought she'd never heard anything sound so good, his deep chuckle rumbling pleasantly in her ears. "I've only known you two days and you've tried to break my nose with a suitcase and drown me in my own pool. I'd be afraid to be around when you decide to really cut loose."

Laura's mouth pulled into a smile.

Some of the tension seeming to ease from his shoulders, Adam started back up the ladder. "You know if you hang around here, I might put you to work," he warned.

"Try me. I'm a pretty good gofer. I know the difference between a socket wrench and a C-clamp."

"I wasn't thinking of anything that technical. Just hand me a few more of those nails, will you?"

He indicated a small box left balanced on the veranda railing. Laura perched her bag beside it and scooped out a few of the nails.

Handing them up to Adam, she stepped back to watch him pound the last board into place.

"What are you doing here, anyway?" she shouted above the thud of the hammer.

"Covering up some of the cracks in the sheathing to keep out moisture until I can do a better job of matching up this old wood."

"Is this place yours?"

"Nope. It belongs to Xavier Storm."

Laura blinked, certain she couldn't have heard him right. "Storm? I didn't think you were on such good terms with him that you'd be helping him fix up his house."

Adam leapt down from the ladder. "I'm not. But just because I don't like the man doesn't mean I can't still care about the lady he abandoned." He chucked her playfully under the chin, giving her one of those lazy smiles that seemed to curl right through her.

"Are you talking about me or the house?" Laura asked indignantly.

"In this case, the house. Storm would like to level this grand old lady and half the town, too, if he could get away with it."

"Level this lovely old place? Then you're working here without his permission?"

"Not exactly. Storm knows I've started taking steps to preserve the house. He thinks I'm a fool, but as long as it's not his time or money, he doesn't care." Adam shrugged. "You ought to know the way his mind works."

It was a casual remark, perhaps too casual. The subject of her supposed past relationship with Storm had ever been a sore point between them.

"I told you I wasn't that close to the man," Laura protested. "And I can't believe anyone would buy this beautiful old house just to destroy it."

"Storm would." Adam gestured back toward the harbor. "He's been buying up property all along here for some development scheme. Exclusive high-rise condos for bored, rich yuppies, who think it's chic to despise the more crowded sea resorts."

"Then why are you working so hard to fix up the house if Storm's going to tear it down?"

"Because I'm going to stop him." Adam's lips thinned into a smile, but the look in his eyes was pure steel, that stubborn resolve Laura had come to know so well. "Storm caught me napping. For years I've been so busy with Barnhart Shipping, I stopped paying attention to what was going on back here at Belle's Point, kind of forgot about this place. The auction for this property was over before I even knew about it."

"If Storm already owns the place, I don't see what you can do."

Adam didn't say anything for a moment; then he angled her a long, measuring look. He still didn't trust her, and there was no reason he should. But the thought brought a real ache to her heart. Everything she'd experienced in Adam's arms, the tenderness, the awareness, the sense of closeness that went beyond mere desire, was apparently all one-sided.

Then he said slowly, "I have documents back at the beach house, old deeds with a peculiar clause in them. Strangely enough, all this property once belonged to my great-grandfather. When he parceled off the land for the first time, he stipulated that the property should never be sold to anyone who didn't live in Belle's Point. The sale to Storm may be illegal, and somehow I can't see him abandoning his jet-set life-style to move here."

"But will such an old clause hold up in court?" Laura asked anxiously.

"I don't know. Failing that, maybe the arts council can help me have this place declared an historic landmark. One can only hope." The look in Adam's eyes told Laura more than words exactly how much hoping he'd been doing.

He gathered up his tools and returned them to a battered metal toolbox. After a brief hesitation, he asked without looking at her, "Would . . . would you like to see inside the house?"

Laura nodded. As he held out his hand to help her up the slightly wobbly front steps, she was left with a strange feeling that Adam was inviting her to do more than see the house, that he was finally letting her inside, letting her draw closer to the man who was Adam Barnhart, than he ever had before.

He unlocked the heavy dead bolt on the front door and ushered her over the threshold, his manner a curious combination of pride and fierce protectiveness. As Laura followed him from room to room, she exclaimed over the carved moldings, ran her hand lovingly over the oak banister curving up to the second floor, sighed over the glorious fireplace that Adam had partly stripped, finding traces of gold-leaf tracery beneath. She hardly needed him to point out the possibilities beyond the cracking plaster and faded wallpaper, her mind keeping pace with his.

By the time they returned to the front porch, they were debating color schemes to be used in the drawing room. As Adam locked up, he remarked with a wry grin, "We sound like two newlyweds setting up housekeeping."

Newlyweds who had come close to kicking off their honeymoon last night. It stunned Laura to realize how little it would take for her to fall into Adam's arms and finish what they had started at poolside. Heat threatened to steal into her cheeks, and she walked to the edge of the veranda fanning herself with her hand.

A nice breeze had started to drift up from the bay. Adam stepped over to join her. He gazed out over the lawn, hands planted on his hips. "I've often thought this would be a great place to live year-round, raise half a dozen kids."

Laura's heart echoed a silent agreement. She could easily imagine it, herself seated on a porch swing with her sketchbook, several towheaded children romping in the front yard, swarming all over Adam when his car pulled into the drive.

"Daddy's home! Daddy's home!"

While the boys clung to his long legs, Adam would hoist the little girl up into his strong arms. Laura would rise from the swing to greet him. His eyes would soften as they met hers, hazy with the promise of moments to be savored later when the children were in bed. Moments on a soft rug in front of the gold-leaf fireplace.

Laura shivered and turned away, rubbing her arms, the vision too poignantly real, too appealing. She was glad that

Adam could not possibly read her foolish thoughts. Her reactions unnerved her. When had it happened, this shift in her feelings toward Adam? She'd stopped thinking of him as pirate, spy, a menace to her sister's happiness, and started envisioning him as friend, husband . . . lover.

To cover her confusion, she cleared her throat and said, "You know an awful lot about Victorian houses for a business executive, Barnhart."

"I didn't grow up wanting to be president of a shipping company. That was Jack's ambition. He was the real whiz kid in the family. It was Jack who built the company up, brought it into the twentieth century."

It seemed to Laura that Adam rarely spoke about his brother, but when he did, it was always about what Jack had wanted, *his* accomplishments, *his* children.

"And what did *you* want to be, Adam?" she asked.

She thought he might brush off the question as he usually did any talk of himself. But he said with an offhand shrug, "Oh, I guess I vaguely remember graduating with a degree in architecture."

Perhaps Laura should have been surprised, but she wasn't. It all fit with some of the remarks Adam had made, personally assuring Laura that the beach house was there to stay.

"Your mother really meant it when she said you built the house for her," she said. "You designed it."

"It's not something to brag about."

"Yes, it is. It's like you got into your mother's head. The house reflects her, so bright, breezy and modern, even a little eccentric."

"That sums up Lou all right."

Laura glanced quickly away to hide a smile, but Adam caught it.

"Now what's that grin for?" he demanded.

"I was just thinking about what I—" Laura broke off to amend quickly. "About what L.C. does in her books. She turns people she knows into rabbits. You turn them into houses."

"Except the beach house is the only place I ever built. There's not much time for that sort of thing when you're knee-deep in shipping invoices."

His voice vibrated through Laura, haunting her with its tone of regret and longing. She understood better now why Adam had been so crazed about Luke being turned aside from his musical gifts.

Adam leaned up against the veranda rail and stared out toward the bay, as if it were his own dreams he could see drifting out with the tide, forever out of reach.

The shipping company was one more thing Adam had inherited from his brother and needed to learn to let go of, Laura thought. But she was not sure he was ready to hear that. Linking her arm through his, she sighed and rested her head against his arm.

Adam glanced down at the glossy crown of her dark braids, woven to rest in a coil along the delicate nape of her neck. She seemed somehow softer, more gentle today in that old-fashioned camisole top, and more stirringly seductive than ever. He could feel the warmth of her cheek where it rested against his arm, could feel just as strongly her silent understanding.

He remembered how she'd been inside the house, her heart-shaped face flushed with excitement, her eyes sparkling. It was as if she'd seen what he'd seen when he looked at those bare walls, as if she'd shared his visions. There had never been anyone who could do that before, not even Jack.

She touched him, delighted him, confused him as no woman ever had. Vague suspicions about her kept flitting into his head, so fantastic he had to dismiss them. But there was something about Chelsey Stuart that just didn't add up, hadn't from the beginning. Her freewheeling life-style was almost a mockery of his own. So why did he keep feeling as if he'd found some sort of kindred spirit?

He turned her slowly to face him, and bent forward to kiss her, merely sipping at her lips. The taste of her mouth was warm and sweet, honeysuckle and sunshine, rose petals and soft sea breezes. It was a kiss more tender than any they had ever shared, and it left him strangely shaken.

When Adam drew back, Laura emitted a soft sigh of protest. Their eyes held for a long moment, the spell broken only by a playful breeze that sent her pink plastic bag tumbling from where she had left it on the porch rail.

"You'd better watch out. There goes your—" Adam broke off, staring at the lacy object that drifted near his foot.

Laura's cheeks fired with dismay. She'd all but forgotten her recent purchases. Now they were spilling out of the bag and across the porch floor for Adam's inspection.

Laura darted forward, but Adam was quicker than she. He scooped up a pair of panties, a wicked confection of rose satin and black lace. As he turned the garment over in his hands, Laura braced herself for some ribald joke.

But none came. The delicate fabric snagged against the rough texture of his fingers. She saw a faint flush creep up his neck, the muscles of his throat working beneath his open collar. The sight of her intimate apparel caught in Adam's strong, tanned hands roused strange sensations in her, a sweet heaviness that matched the look settling into his eyes.

He expelled a long breath. "Damn. This is enough to make me wish I'd started my reconstruction with one of the bedrooms."

His gaze met hers with a flash like heat lightning. Laura felt the quickening of her own response. Did they really need a bedroom?

This startling thought was dispelled by the blare of a car horn. Laura felt almost as if someone had wagged an admonishing finger at her.

Springing a little away from Adam, she saw a sleek black limo on the street below. It pulled impatiently around an old man on a bicycle, then eased closer to the curb.

"Sonofabitch!"

The flare in Adam's eyes had turned to fire of a different sort. His entire frame seemed to go taut.

"What is it?" Laura asked.

"Not what, who," Adam growled. "Don't you recognize the license plate on that car?"

Laura glanced back toward the bumper of the limo. The black letters stood out clearly beneath the logo of the Garden State. Letters that spelled out a single, daunting word.

Storm.

Seven

The letters of the license plate seemed to brand themselves on Laura's mind, as black as the headline she'd seen recently, as ominous as the key word those reporters had buzzed in her ears.

Storm.

Rooted to the spot, Laura watched a burly chauffeur get out of the limo. With a physique that would have done credit to Conan the Barbarian and a face that would have looked at home on a post-office wall, it was obvious that he functioned as more than a driver.

He ambled to open the back door of the limo and a tall man with waves of midnight-colored hair emerged, his lean features shadowed behind the anonymity of dark sunglasses. On the back street of this quiet town, Xavier Storm appeared somewhat larger than life, with his expensive three-piece silk suit and sleek movie-idol looks.

Laura had never met the man, but she recognized him from the papers and clips from the evening news. Storm arrogantly waving away the press, Storm cutting a ribbon on his newest hotel complex, Storm denying his development projects were doing anything to threaten salt-marsh wildlife. Storm, multimillionaire, ruthless entrepreneur, Adam's adversary and . . . Chelsey Stuart's ex-lover.

It was this last thought that caused Laura's stomach to tighten with apprehension. So far she had squeaked by with her impersonation of Chelsey. But she hadn't played out the part for anyone who actually knew her sister, certainly not a man who had been acquainted with Chelsey on more intimate terms than Laura liked to think about.

Hardly aware she did so, Laura clutched at Adam's arm. "Adam," she whispered, as if Storm could overhear her even from the street. "What's he doing here?"

"I don't know. I didn't think the man ever emerged from his coffin in the daylight."

Despite Adam's dry humor, Laura sensed the tension coursing through him, a tension that matched her own racing heart. She wondered how Adam would react to the suggestion they just make a bolt for it. Probably think she was crazy, and it was too late, anyway.

Storm was already striding through the wrought-iron gate. Laura had known some wealthy men who walked as if they expected all the world to bow down to them. Storm moved as if he expected the world to get out of his way.

Laura had a sinking feeling that the twelve-hour extension she had given Chelsey was about to come to an abrupt end. She resisted the urge to duck behind Adam as Storm approached the front steps.

He paused to glance up at Laura and Adam, his face seeming more lean than it had on television, all hollows and angles, his mouth having an arrogant curve.

"Well, well," he said. "Mr. Barnhart, isn't it? The crusading boat builder. Still plying your hammer?"

"That's right." Adam placed his hands on his hips, his whole stance one of stubborn challenge. "Going to have me arrested?"

"For what? Making unwanted home repairs?" Storm's voice had a low, purring quality. "I told you before that I understood. Entertainment must be damned hard to come by in this neck of the woods, if you have to work at restoring houses destined for the wrecking ball." Storm's attention shifted to Laura. "Although it seems you finally found something else to amuse you."

Adam glared and said, "I suppose I don't have to introduce you to Chelsey Stuart."

"Chelsey?"

Laura heard the doubt in Storm's voice and squirmed. Was it only her imagination or was the man behind those impenetrable dark lenses mentally undressing her, trying to decide if she really was the woman he'd once had in bed? Say something clever, she thought desperately, to establish your identity before Storm has a chance to question it. Forcing a smile to her lips, she said, "Hello, Xavier."

"Xavier?" he echoed.

Laura's heart sank, aware from his tone that she had erred. What on earth had Chelsey called the man? Storm didn't seem the sort for Chelsey's usual nicknames of "hon" or "kiddo."

"Long time, no see," Laura concluded weakly.

Brilliant, Laura. She swallowed a groan. Storm stared at her. He definitely possessed an unfair advantage, the dark tint of his glasses masking his thoughts. But forget the sunglasses. At this moment, Laura would have given anything for a brown paper bag to have pulled over her head.

After what seemed an eternity, Storm finally murmured, "It's been a long time, Chelsey. I would've hardly recognized you. This is quite a new look—from Madonna to Pollyanna."

"I—I've been helping Adam with the house," Laura said.

"And I see you've been going at it from the bottom up."

Storm's faintly amused comment made no sense until Laura realized that Adam was still clutching a pair of her new lacy panties in his hand. Laura gave a horrified gasp and felt her face flood with heat. Adam pulled a wry face and stuffed the undergarment in Laura's shopping bag.

"So what brings you down from your penthouse, Storm?" Adam demanded. "I thought you had at least a hundred flunkies to run your errands for you."

"True, but occasionally I do descend myself. Just to see firsthand the downtrodden masses I'm accused of oppressing. You aroused my curiosity about this house you're moving heaven and earth to save. I'd hate to think there's something of value here I'm missing."

Storm strolled past Adam. Tipping back his head, he examined the house at a languid pace, his lips pursing slightly. Why, Laura wondered, with Storm here, did the flaws in the lovely, old house suddenly seem more glaringly apparent, the peeling paint, the missing molding, the rotted boards? Running well-manicured fingertips over the gingerbread trim adorning a window, Storm grimaced when a piece broke off in his hand. He extended the wooden shard toward Adam.

"Sorry. I suppose you'll be wanting to preserve this for posterity, too."

Adam wrenched the shard of wood from Storm's hand. "I don't think you'd want to know what I'd really like to do with this," he said.

Although Storm laughed, Laura cringed. Adam's manner was far from compromising. If there was a chance that Storm might be swayed, Adam, in his stubbornness, was throwing it away. Laura didn't know how much influence Chelsey had possessed with Storm, if any. But if the exercise of some her sister's charm would help Adam, Laura had to be bold enough to try.

Swallowing hard, she crossed over to Storm. She rested her hand lightly on his arm, forcing a Chelseylike smile to her lips.

"Wouldn't you like to see the inside of the house before you make up your mind, Mr. Storm . . . Xavier—uh, hon?"

Laura didn't know what seemed to astonish the man more, her appeal or her use of the endearment. Discomfited, she removed her hand from his sleeve.

"There appears to be a lock on the front door," Storm said.

"I put that there," Adam said. "Someone had to make an effort to keep out vandals."

"How prudent. But I doubt it will have much effect against bulldozers. The lock looks quite valuable. I'll see that you get it back when the house comes down."

"That will be decided in court."

"No, I assure you. You'll get the lock back whether the judge orders me to do so or not."

Adam's response to Storm's wit was a smile that was dangerously thin. It frightened Laura how well she could read Adam's mind, his growing desire to seize Storm by the collar of his expensive suit and send him flying headfirst off the porch. Then that gorilla of Storm's in the chauffeur's uniform would likely tear Adam apart.

Laura stepped hastily in between Storm and Adam. She continued to coax Storm, "You've come so far to see this place. You could at least take a better look. If you would just let us show you the inside—"

"I'm afraid not," Storm interrupted. "I've never been much for the joys of fading wallpaper and inadequate indoor plumbing."

"But this house is part of our country's architectural heritage."

"So are outhouses. But that's no reason we should try to save them all."

"But if you would only—"

"Forget it, Chelsey." This time it was Adam who interrupted her. "Mr. Storm wouldn't recognize real elegance if he tripped over it. Just look at those concrete elephants he builds and calls hotels. You're wasting your breath with him."

"Just as I have been wasting my time here." Storm shifted back his coat sleeve and consulted his Rolex. "However, it was lucky my running into you, Chelsey. It gives me a chance to settle some unfinished business between us."

Laura stiffened. Was she imagining it or had Storm's smile suddenly taken on a predatory gleam?

"Wh-what unfinished business?" Laura stammered.

"Chelsey," he said softly, stalking closer. "Surely you haven't forgotten so soon."

"Well, I—I—" She cast a desperate look toward Adam. He folded his arms across his chest, his eyes dark with... suspicion? Betrayal? Laura winced as she remembered how much time she had spent reassuring Adam there was nothing between her and Xavier Storm.

Laura backed up until she felt the porch rail press against her spine. "Our relationship was all very casual, wasn't it? Just a few dates."

"A few dates?" Storm repeated.

Laura racked her mind in vain for anything Chelsey might have said about Storm to help her handle this situation. "After all, you're still a married man."

"My divorce is almost final."

"But—but whatever spark there was between us is over."

"Is it?" Slowly he removed his sunglasses. Laura was dismayed to see that it didn't help. He had tigerish green eyes hooded beneath deep lids. She still couldn't read his thoughts.

"Yes," she continued. "Even if you are getting divorced, you—you shouldn't go chasing off on the rebound."

"You make me sound like a demented basketball."

Listening to this exchange, Adam felt a strange mix of emotions churn in his gut. He wondered if he would ever understand Chelsey Stuart. With her reputation, she ought to have been able to deal with a man like Storm, put him in his place as easily as dismissing a cur to its kennel. And yet strangely Chelsey seemed as defenseless against Storm's aggression as that old house would be against his bulldozers. A fierce surge of jealousy and protectiveness coursed through Adam.

Although he felt about as Neanderthal as some ridiculous caveman, he couldn't seem to help himself. He stalked close to Chelsey and slipped his arm possessively about her shoulders.

"I think the lady is trying to tell you she's no longer interested, Storm," Adam said.

"Yes, that's it," Laura's sigh was almost grateful. "That's exactly what I was trying to say."

Rather than looking annoyed, Storm appeared more amused than ever. "What? No longer interested in pursuing her photographic career?"

"What the hell are you talking about?" Adam growled.

"Can it be that Chelsey never told you why we got to know each other in the first place?"

Adam directed a questioning look at Laura. She bit down on her lip and toyed nervously with her braid. How or why Chelsey had become involved with Storm, Laura had no idea. Her sister just seemed able to pull men out of a hat the way magicians did rabbits.

For once Storm decided to be helpful and explain. "I saw some of Chelsey's pictures at a local art exhibit. I thought she had talent and offered to use my influence to get her a job working for a major New York magazine."

"Oh, that," Laura said weakly.

"You disappointed me, Chelsey, disappearing that way, after I had gone to so much trouble on your behalf. The editor at *She* magazine is still waiting for the rest of your portfolio. I suppose you have been too busy—er—*refinishing* with Mr. Barnhart."

"The editor will get the damned pictures, Storm," Adam snapped.

"By next week," Laura added.

"That won't do, Chelsey. You need to have them in as soon as possible. I will be having dinner with the publisher of *She* tomorrow night. You need to send me the photographs by then."

Laura sighed. What was she supposed to say? How could she make promises on her sister's behalf. She didn't know if this job at *She* magazine was that important to Chelsey. Chelsey had once talked of moving to New York, becoming a professional photographer. But the sad truth was that Laura knew so little about what Chelsey wanted these days—except for Luke Barnhart.

"Well..." Laura paused. "I think Chels—that is, I think I have some good shots of the coast by Ocean City in my portfolio back at the beach house."

Storm's silky laugh caused the hairs on the back of her neck to prickle. "Ah, Chelsey. Always the kidder. Of course, you know what is needed. Some rather candid shots celebrating the beauties of the naked masculine form."

"Beefcake photos," Adam interpreted flatly, arching one brow in Laura's direction.

She cringed. Photographs of naked men? Merciful heavens, what next!

"By tomorrow afternoon," Storm pressed.

Laura bit down on her lip. "I—I couldn't possibly. I mean, that's not enough time."

"But this is the opportunity of a lifetime, my dear," Storm purred. "I can't believe that after I went to such trouble on your behalf—"

"She'll get the damn pictures to you," Adam snapped.

Laura wanted the ground to open up and swallow her. She angled Adam a glance, partly indignant, partly desperate. Whose side was he on, anyway?

But before she could protest any further, Storm accepted the matter as settled. "I'll be working at my office until four," he said. "Have the photos to me by then."

Settling his sunglasses back into place, Storm started down the porch steps. He only paused to flash one last smile. "Do you know I'm glad I came, after all? I never imagined visiting decrepit old houses could prove this entertaining."

Laura watched Storm's retreat with simmering resentment. His face was quite bland as he eased into the limo. But she had the oddest feeling the damn man was going to laugh the whole way back to Atlantic City.

As Storm's limo swung out from the curb, Laura could hardly bring herself to turn and face Adam, certain that he must be placing the worst possible interpretation on what had just passed between her and Xavier Storm.

When she did dare to glance his way, it was to find Adam gathering up his toolbox. Any trace of the warmth, the laughter, the understanding they had shared before Storm's arrival seemed to have vanished. Laura's heart sank.

"We'd better be getting back to the beach house. You appear to have a busy afternoon ahead of you, Miss Stuart," he said.

"Adam, I'm not going to take those pictures."

"Why not? You don't want to miss your big opportunity, do you? Especially not after you obviously expended great effort with Mr. Storm to bring all this about."

She flinched at the sarcastic bite in his tone. "Chels—that is, I didn't sleep with Storm to advance my career. I don't do things like that."

"I never said you did."

"But you were thinking it."

"You don't have the least idea what I'm thinking."

That was true and it was making Laura uncomfortable, as uncomfortable as the odd, speculative way Adam kept staring at her.

"If this job of Storm's is something you've always dreamed of," he said, "I guess you'd better go for it."

"Well, I—I can't. I don't even have my photographic equipment with me."

"Yes, you do. I saw your camera bag when I helped Luke unload the trunk."

"And where would I take pictures like—like *that?* In your family's living room?"

"That would be a real treat for Lou. But, no, I think you'd better do your shoot on the beach. It's nice and private there."

Laura moistened her lips nervously. What was the matter with Adam? It was as if he were trying to goad her into this as much as Storm had done.

"And just how am I supposed to come up with a model?" she asked. "Go up to some passing fisherman here at the point and ask if he'd like to strip for me?"

"I wouldn't recommend that. You'd be likely to get too many volunteers." Adam stared out toward the bay, his gray eyes dark and thoughtful. After another heartbeat of hesitation, he said, "No, I'll do it."

"Do what?"

"Pose for you."

Laura gaped at him, wondering if he had accidently hit himself in the head with his own hammer.

"You?" she breathed. "You would be willing to pose for me?"

"Yes."

"N-naked?"

"Why not? You've been telling me how natural it is."

"But—but—"

"That is, unless you don't think I would do?" he challenged.

Laura gulped. That was the problem. She did think Adam would do, all too well. Since she'd met the man, she'd been tormented with dozens of shocking fantasies of Adam unclothed, but they all concerned him holding her tenderly, passionately in his arms, not displaying himself like some—some male stripper for the cold eye of Chelsey's camera.

Wiping at the beads of perspiration that had gathered on her brow, she choked out a reply, "Of course I think you would be great naked— That is, I mean, you're very— But surely you wouldn't want to—to—"

"Why not?" Adam shrugged. "Maybe I have allowed myself to get a little too stiff-necked and uptight. But knowing you has loosened me up considerably."

Laura shook her head. "I don't believe it. You're the most private man I've ever met. You told me that you hate being photographed, that it's like baring your soul."

"But it's not my soul I'm planning to bare for you," Adam said with a hard, wicked smile. "I'll take you back to the house and meet you down on the beach as soon as I've changed."

Changed into what? As Laura watched Adam's retreat down the porch steps, she was too horrified to ask.

Laura spent the next hour pacing the Barnharts' kitchen, jabbing out the phone number of the cousins in Hammonton and trying not to panic. She finally reached a bored ten-year-old who dragged himself away from his video games long enough to inform Laura that Luke and Chelsey had gone off to some kind of picnic at the lake.

Picnic? Laura thought as she replaced the phone in its cradle. That didn't sound as if Chelsey were laying any heavy revelations on Luke. But Laura had told her sister that she could have until nine o'clock tonight. Trust Chelsey to put the unpleasant moment off until one last minute.

But this whole situation had finally gone beyond impossible. Laura hardly knew one end of the camera from another. She couldn't have faked being a professional photographer even if her subject was something like—like an adorable, fuzzy puppy. But when her model was going to be Adam in all his naked glory...

A shiver of the most wicked anticipation coursed through Laura. She quelled it, thinking she ought to be ashamed of herself. Besides she was worrying and quivering for nothing. Adam was only goading her. He surely wouldn't go through with this. Not really. Would he?

Laura fretted her lower lip as she remembered the drive home from Belle's Point. Adam had said little, but the look in his eyes had been pure steel. Why would he even volunteer to do something like this? If it hadn't all sounded so crazy, Laura would have suspected the man was out to prove something.

She knew he had already gone down to the beach. She had heard the door slam while she was busy trying to get her call connected. He was probably pacing the sand, waiting for her even now.

In his birthday suit? Laura gave a small, wistful moan and dragged her hand back through her bangs. Oh, what a time for the man's mother to be off playing golf. But even if Lou Barnhart had been here, she probably would have just passed Adam the suntan oil and told him to have fun.

Well, it didn't matter. Laura pressed her hands to her face, trying to calm herself. Short of breaking her promise to Chelsey and telling Adam everything, she would find some other way out of this.

Soothing herself with that vague thought, Laura let herself out the back door and headed away from the house, down toward the beach. Her sandals sank into the deep, warm sand.

The beach was as private as Adam had promised, at this late hour of the afternoon. Nothing but surf, sky and a shore so untamed, dunes and wild marsh grass shifted in the stiff afternoon breeze.

Appearing out of place in the middle of all this wild, natural beauty stood the Barnharts' cabana, the gaudy red-and-white canvas structure looking like the tent of some desert sheikh. Adam was already there, waiting. Any hope she'd had that he might make things easier for her and back down from this nonsense quickly died. Even from this distance, she knew that look of stubborn determination.

He had changed into a gray hooded sweatshirt and a pair of formfitting cutoffs. The taut denim hugged the sleek muscles of his derriere and thighs, leaving little to Laura's imagination.

But then, if she didn't think up a good excuse, fast, to get herself out of this, she wasn't going to need any imagination at all where Adam was concerned.

Adam Barnhart. Stripped to the buff. The thought had a powerful effect on her. Hot flashes and cold sweats. The fire in her veins warring with the chills of her nervous embarrassment. Was it possible, she wondered, for a woman to be lascivious and prudish at the same time?

Stumbling a little in the shifting sand, she covered the remaining distance between them. She found she couldn't look Adam in the eye. But lowering her gaze was equally unsettling. Those faded denims of his were really well worn, frayed and threadbare in some spots, revealing patches of tanned thigh sugared with fine gold hair.

What in the world did one say to a man one was supposed to photograph buck naked?

"Hi." Laura managed a weak smile, awkwardly stuffing her hand in the pocket of her jeans.

"You're late," he said.

"I—I had to take care of a few things." Like checking on flights to Mexico, praying for a hurricane, a tidal wave, anything to stall for time.

"The light's already starting to fade. We'd better get started," Adam said. He seemed prepared to get down to business with the same briskness he might have conducted a board meeting.

"Oh, darn!" Laura said, attempting to snap her fingers. Her middle finger slushed against her damp palm. "I forgot my camera bag, after all."

"That's all right. I fetched it for you while you were busy on the phone."

Laura gritted her teeth as she saw Chelsey's huge vinyl camera bag propped near the cabana. The man was being so damned helpful. He was going to help her straight to a nervous breakdown. When Adam started to strip off his sweatshirt, Laura experienced a fluttering of panic.

"Wait," she cried, grabbing his wrist to stop him. When he gave her a cool, questioning look, she stammered, "Um, perhaps this isn't such a good idea. That breeze coming off the ocean. *Brrr.*" She affected a deep shiver. "I wouldn't want you to—um—catch a cold."

"Don't worry about me. I've got Norse blood in my veins."

He seized the hem of his sweatshirt and started to tug again.

"No," Laura cried. "Uh—that is, the light isn't ideal. We could do this another day. Perhaps tomorrow."

"No, we can't. You heard what Storm said. You need to send in your portfolio by tomorrow or you'll miss your chance." Adam shot her an impatient glance. Since she kept preventing him from removing his shirt, he kicked off his leather thongs instead.

Laura persisted, "I just don't want you to—to do anything that might make you uncomfortable."

"Who's uncomfortable? You seem to be having more trouble with this than I am, Chelsey."

"I'm not. It's just that—" Laura racked her brain for another excuse. "I can't photograph you this way."

"What way?"

"You're too hard."

"Too what?" He exclaimed incredulously.

Her eyes flicked to the bulge in the front of his denims.

"Oh, I—I didn't mean... I only meant you seem too tense."

"There's nothing wrong with my mood. Now are you going to take the damned pictures or not?"

"Fine!" she snapped, her own tension giving way to anger. If he was that keen to parade around naked, who was she to stop him? It wasn't going to upset her. It wasn't as if she were some giggly, bashful teenager.

As for photographing him, Laura had bluffed her way through far worse moments this past weekend. But she was hard pressed to think of any as she unzipped Chelsey's camera bag. Chelsey had three cameras, and Laura was prepared to bet not one of them was an Instamatic.

Laura removed the smallest and most harmless looking one from its case. She turned the 35 mm in her hands as gingerly as if it were a probe from Mars. The rest of the equipment Chelsey had in the bag was just as daunting, some kind of meter, extra lenses, a foil-wrapped packet...

What on earth could that be for? Curious, Laura pulled it out to examine it. When she realized the little packet had nothing to do with photography, her face flamed and she stuffed it back in the bag before Adam saw it.

Finding the condom only added to Laura's discomfiture. She determined not to probe any further into the bag. Who knew what else Chelsey might have in there? Besides, attempting to load the camera would only expose her own ignorance.

There had to be a way she could fake it, pretend that she was taking pictures. Where was the little button that she should click? Every camera had to have a little button, didn't it? As Laura looked for it, a gull wheeled overhead, emitting its strange cry, which sounded like mocking laughter.

"Who asked for your opinion?" she muttered.

"What?" Adam asked.

"Nothing. I—" Glancing up, she broke off with a stifled gasp. Adam had discarded his sweatshirt.

The late-afternoon light bathed his bronzed flesh, the rippling muscle of his shoulders, the smooth power of his upper arms and chest. Heat rushed into Laura's cheeks.

With the sun gleaming behind him like a ball of fire, the sea at his back, the wind riffling his dark blond hair, there was something raw and primitive about him.

And Laura's response was equally primitive. She felt desire stir in her as timeless as the rhythm of the sea. Moistening her lips, she swallowed hard. She remembered she'd once asked Chelsey how anyone could possibly film naked men without blushing.

"It's only another job," Chelsey had shrugged. "You just keep it impersonal."

But Laura's reactions to Adam Barnhart had never been impersonal. Not from the very beginning. She didn't even realize she was devouring the sight of him until their eyes met, his own taking on the sudden, smoky haze of awareness. His hands moved slowly to the button fly of his cutoffs. Laura stared at the taut, flat plane of his stomach, the dusting of golden hairs that disappeared so intriguingly beneath the waistband.

"Perhaps we should start with a few waist-up shots first," she suggested.

"All right." Adam's own voice sounded a little huskier. "Where do you want me?"

Here. Now. The thought startled Laura as much as the unexpected ache of longing that accompanied it.

"Where you are is just fine." She sought refuge behind the camera, trying to find detachment through the lens. Circling around Adam, she fiddled with knobs, twisting this, clicking that, attempting to look as if she knew what she was doing.

"Don't you want me to do anything?" Adam asked.

"Well, I..." Laura focused momentarily on his hands, those lean, strong, deft fingers. She remembered the way they had felt when Adam had kissed her, threading through her hair, stroking her back, cupping her breast.

"N-no," she quavered. "Just act casual."

It would be good if at least one of them could.

"Don't you want the rest of my clothes off?"

She couldn't answer. She wanted to shout, "No!" but she feared her eyes must be communicating the opposite. It wasn't nice, she admonished herself, wanting to look at a man naked.

But she didn't want to look at just any man. Only Adam. She felt as shameless as any voyeur as she watched Adam's hand drop to his denims, his fingers easing open the first button of his fly.

As he moved onto the next, Laura shuddered and managed to wrench her eyes away. She turned her back, pretending to be furiously absorbed with the camera. The beach seemed to be as tense and quiet as she was, the silence broken only by the endless crashing of the waves, the cries of the seabirds.

She sensed Adam stalking over to stand behind her. She straightened to a rigid posture, almost imagining she could feel the heat emanating from his now-naked body. His voice came, raspy and low, so close by her ear, she could feel the warmth of his breath tickle her neck.

"As long as I'm going to the bother of stripping, Chelsey, I have a suggestion to make."

"Y-yes?" she faltered, feeling as if her knees were about to turn to water.

"Maybe you ought to take the lens cap off the camera."

The suggestion was so different from what she had expected, it took a moment for Adam's remark to compute.

"The lens cap?" she repeated stupidly. Glancing down, she was mortified to see the black plastic still covering the lens of the camera. Her gaze skittered involuntarily back toward Adam.

He hadn't removed his cutoffs after all. She didn't know whether she was more relieved or disappointed. Somehow she lost her hold on the camera, dropping it into the sand.

"Oh, damn," she said, bending down to retrieve it, realizing how badly her hands were shaking.

Adam hunkered down beside her, his bare knee brushing against her thigh. He took the camera from her, examining it, dusting away the sand.

"I don't think you broke it," he said.

"I hope not." Laura sought for some excuse for her awkward behavior. "I'm not usually this clumsy. I don't know what's the matter with me."

"Oh, I think I do."

Laura cast him an uneasy glance.

"There's only one problem with you, Miss Chelsey Stuart." His lips curved into a slow smile.

"You are a complete and utter fraud."

Eight

Laura felt her heart go still.

"Wh-what?" she stuttered.

Adam returned the camera to the bag before answering. He came back to where Laura still crouched, frozen by his words. Running his hands lightly up her arms, he gripped her by the shoulders, raising her up to her feet.

"I said you are a fraud," he repeated calmly.

So Adam had guessed the truth. She had exposed herself at last. Laura felt almost relieved, until his next words dispelled that illusion.

"You're not what you pretend to be, Chelsey Stuart."

Chelsey. Laura felt her momentary hope plummet. He still thought she was Chelsey. She was as trapped as she had ever been in this crazy masquerade.

He cupped her chin, forcing her to look up, his own eyes intent, as if he meant to peer all the way into the depths of her soul. "For all your casual talk about nudity and sex, I think you hold the same old-fashioned values as I do. You didn't want to take naked pictures of me for that ridiculous magazine any more than I wanted to pose for them."

"So you were only testing me," Laura accused. "You never meant to go through with it."

"I guess I would've if I thought you really wanted me to."

"Why?"

"Because the thought of you hanging around here on the beach with some other naked man makes me a little crazy." His lips tipped into a rueful smile. "And, yes, maybe I was testing you. You've confused me since the moment I first met you. It's almost as if you're two different women."

Laura stole a glance at her watch. Five o'clock. What difference could four more hours possibly make to Chelsey? Promise or no promise, Laura couldn't endure this any longer.

Summoning up her courage, she said, "Adam, there's something I have to explain to you—"

But he brushed his fingertips lightly over her lips, silencing her. "You don't have to explain anything to me. I understand."

"Y-you do?"

"For whatever reason, you think you have to put on a facade of being this hard, sexy, modern woman. But it isn't necessary. You're vibrant and desirable enough without all this pretense."

Laura Stuart vibrant and desirable? Oh, God, if he only knew. Laura felt herself dying a little inside as Adam continued tenderly, "Basically, I believe you're too honest a person for these games."

Too honest? Laura gulped. The confession she was trying to make lodged like a hot ball in her throat.

"And you don't need the help of a man like Storm. If you're as talented as I think you are, you can make it on your own. You need to watch out for him, Chelsey. He never does any favors for anyone without a pretty hefty price tag attached."

"I told you, Adam," Laura managed to find her voice at last, "there's never been anything between me and Storm. There never will be."

"Good. You're not Storm's kind of woman."

Her heart pounded madly as his arms slid around her waist.

"Then what kind of a woman do you think I am?" she asked sadly.

"Mine."

He drew her against his bare chest. She could feel his heat even through the cotton of her blouse. He tangled his hand in her hair, his mouth poised over hers for a heartbeat. Then he claimed her with a kiss that was gentle and possessive, as if Adam sought to reclaim the tenderness they had shared before Storm's arrival had cast a shadow over everything.

Laura melted against him, her lips parting beneath his assault, inviting his possession. When his tongue invaded her mouth in all its hot sweetness, she moaned deep in her throat.

He tempered the rising passion of his kiss to become more gentle, to taste of her lips, her chin, her eyelids, her hair. With a deep, shuddering sigh, he rested his forehead against her own.

"Chelsey," he murmured, "I want to make love to you. I never wanted anything more in my life."

No. It wasn't her he wanted. Adam didn't even know her name. But did that really matter? Laura wondered wistfully. When she was in Adam's arms, she wasn't the circumspect L.C. Stuart, lady children's author. She was a different woman altogether, a little daring, a little reckless, for once not stopping to count the cost of her actions or even to think. Only to need, to feel the delicious sensation Adam stirred inside of her.

Wrapping her arms about his neck, pressing herself more closely against the length of him, Laura heard her own reply, "I want you, too, Adam."

She kissed him, teasing her tongue along the texture of his lips, both shocked and delighted by her own boldness. A shudder coursed through Adam, and he kissed her back with a feverish intensity.

His hands roved over her back, coming down to cup her bottom, holding her so hard against him, she could feel the extent of his arousal. An answering need throbbed to life inside her.

She arched her neck as Adam's lips roamed downward, caressing the column of her throat, the heat of his mouth settling over her madly beating pulse. He slipped his hands beneath the delicate white eyelet of her blouse. Laura shivered as the rough warmth of his hands made contact with her bare flesh, his fingers stroking upward to the curve of her bra.

She felt her breasts go taut with anticipation. But to her amazement and disappointment, he checked the motion. Groaning, he wrenched himself away from her.

"Oh, God, Chelsey," he panted. "We can't. Not here. Not now. I—I've got no way of protecting you."

Protecting her from what? It took Laura a moment to comprehend his meaning. Protection. How many men besides Adam would be gallant enough to stop and think of such a thing in the middle of a rush of passion?

His concern for her touched and frustrated Laura. He couldn't know how rare for her this moment was. Tomorrow she would wake up and find herself back to being Laura Stuart, a woman far too inhibited to ever admit how much she wanted Adam and wanted to make love to him on a windswept beach. This magic might never touch her again.

She considered flinging herself back into the shelter of his arms, attempting to override Adam's scruples when a thought struck her.

"Wait a moment," she murmured, darting away from him.

His desire for her feeling like a red-hot flame burning in his loins, Adam drew in deep breaths. He watched her movements, mystified when she removed something from the camera bag, then returned to him, looking adorably flustered.

"I don't want you to think— But it just so happens that I—" She thrust forward one fist, slowly opening it. "Here."

Adam's eyes widened when he saw what she had cupped in her hand. His lips curved in a slow, incredulous smile.

"Well, you certainly came prepared."

"But I didn't. I don't want you to think that I planned this—" she said, clearly distressed by his teasing. "That I go around doing this sort of thing with everyone I photograph."

"I don't. Any more than I offer to strip for every female photographer who comes strolling down the beach."

"But I know you think I make a habit of—"

He silenced her by placing his fingertips on her lips.

"I'm not thinking anything just now, except how beautiful you are. No explanations, no excuses are necessary between us, Chelsey. Not about your past. Not about mine."

And he took the foil-wrapped packet from her as solemnly as if it were a gift she offered. He tucked it in the pocket of his cutoffs, then raised her hand lightly to his lips before leading her to the shelter of the cabana.

It was cool and shadowed within the structure, the heavy canvas seeming to shut out the world—even the roar of the ocean was muted. Adam spread out a blanket and Laura sat down, hugging her knees to her chest.

As he eased himself down beside her, her eyes roved over the canvas walls that shifted a little from the force of the wind. She smiled. "This is like something out of *The*

Sheikh. I feel a little like Agnes Ayres being carried off by Rudolph Valentino."

"Only one major difference." He brushed back a stray tendril of hair from her eyes. "I would never take a woman by force."

"I know that, Adam. I don't think I've ever known a man more gentle than you."

The thought flitted through his mind before he could help it. How many men had she known? It wasn't important. All that counted was that she was here now, with him.

Fingering the ends of her long, thick braid, he began to slowly undo the intricate arrangement until her hair fanned about her shoulders in ripples of golden brown. She seemed all of a sudden shy, even nervous.

And though Adam hated to admit it, he felt a little nervous himself. It had been quite a while since he had been willing to risk making a fool of himself over any woman, especially one with Chelsey's reputation for collecting and discarding men.

He'd been determined to mistrust her and the powerful attraction she aroused in him. But for once he couldn't fight his instincts, looking beyond the tabloid pages to the woman he'd discovered these past few days, warm, open and compassionate.

She gazed up at him, her eyes large, luminous and trusting, her lips half parted in invitation. If this was folly, Adam thought as he bent to kiss her, perhaps he had attempted to be wise for far too long. Her hands rested softly on his shoulders, then trailed down to explore the expanse of his chest. Her tentative touch was somehow more arousing than if she had raked her hands over him boldly.

His breath quickening, it was all he could do to control the impatience of his own building desire. He began to unbutton her blouse, forcing himself to go slow. He'd waited too long for this moment to have it come and go in a heated rush.

The fabric of her blouse parted and he slipped it off her shoulders, reveling in the sight of her skin, as pale and smooth as ivory, her collarbone as fragile as the pulse beating at the base of her throat.

Then his gaze drifted down to her bra. It was absurd, but Laura experienced a strong urge to cover herself. If only she had worn some of the daring lingerie she had purchased at Gertie's Garters. Her plain white cotton had to be about as enticing as a teenager's training bra.

As Adam tugged her down to lay beside him, Laura wished she had one tenth of her sister's knowledge about men.

"Oh, Adam," she murmured. "I—I hope I don't disappoint you."

"Funny." He gave a lopsided smile. "I was just thinking the same thing about you. And I want so much to make this good for you, Chelsey."

It stunned her that he could make such an admission, a man as proud and self-confident as Adam. That he could have such self-doubts, be so anxious to please her brought a lump to Laura's throat.

The man was always so—so damned honest.

And what was she offering him in return? Lies. Pretenses. How could she let him make love to her when she was deceiving him this way?

But how could she bear to stop him, either? she thought when Adam kissed her again. His mouth moved over hers, bringing with it a sweet, hot magic that threatened to steal away what little reason she had left.

Was it so wrong to take the risk that Adam would understand when she finally told him the truth, so wrong for once in her life to be just a little selfish?

She could not hold back a blissful sigh as his fingers skimmed over her ribs, his touch brushing her skin like a light sea breeze, spreading a hot languor through her body.

"Oh, Adam," she murmured. "There—there's so much you don't know about me. I don't think—"

"Hush. We both think too much. Let's just let nature take its course."

"But I— Oh!" She gasped as she felt him undo the clasp of her bra, whisking the garment away from her. He held her just close enough so the tips of her breasts barely grazed against him, a torment as exquisite as his kiss. He tugged playfully at her lower lip, the moist heat of his tongue teasing hers.

The last of her scruples vanished when Adam insinuated his fingers between them. How could a woman be expected to cling to her reason when Adam was cupping her breast that way, cradling it in his large, callused hand? Laura groaned as he gently abraded her nipple to a state of pebblelike hardness, only to replace his palm with the hot wetness of his mouth. His tongue dipped and swirled, filling her with a pleasure so intense, it was akin to pain.

The heavy, warm feeling inside her spiraled lower to become an aching need. She buried her hands in his hair, feeling no shame when he began to tug off her jeans, only a growing eagerness.

Adam drew back, drinking in the sight of her nakedness. He wondered how a woman could appear at once so fragile and so seductive, a rosy flush spreading over her pale skin, her hair fanned out like a curtain of silk.

"Chelsey," he whispered. "I know you must have heard this so many times, but you are so beautiful."

Her eyes reflected both disbelief and gratitude.

"Thank you," she said. There was a wistfulness in her voice that affected him strangely. And it occurred to him that Chelsey Stuart could do far more than arouse his body. She was capable of touching his heart.

Kneeling, Adam began impatiently tugging off the rest of his own clothes. Laura watched him through lowered lashes, this time not even tempted to look away.

He was all strength, all lean, hard muscle, so gloriously, unabashedly male. Chelsey had been so right. A man's body could be utterly magnificent.

She must have emitted a tiny murmur of appreciation, because Adam grinned at her.

"Sorry that you didn't take those pictures now?"

She shook her head. "No, I'm too selfish to share you with anyone."

Laura experienced a longing so great it stunned her, a desire to touch, to know every inch of him. But as she reached for him, she was surprised when he did not return immediately to her embrace.

It took her a second before she figured out what he was doing. She heard the crinkle of the foil wrapper and saw a peculiar look pass over Adam's face.

He glanced back at her. "Neon?"

Laura stole a shocked glance. Neon pink to be precise. Only Chelsey, Laura thought. But instead of groaning, she had to stifle a desire to giggle.

"Live dangerously, Mr. Barnhart," she murmured.

He tumbled back down beside her, and Laura felt the rumble of laughter in his chest. It was like one of those foolish jokes only lovers who had long been intimate could share.

Funny that it should be that way. She had known Adam but a few short days. How was it possible that she could feel she had known Adam forever, that their loving could seem as new as a first stolen kiss, as timelessly familiar as if he had been in her arms for eternity?

As he pulled her back into his embrace, all laughter stilled to be replaced by untempered desire. His hands moved over her, stroking her, exploring her, freeing her.

Laura responded by touching him, molding her body to his, moving beneath him, doing, feeling things she had never known she was capable of. She scarce recognized herself in the lover who moaned and moved with such abandon in Adam's arms.

She loved the smooth, hard feel of his skin, the sweet, hot taste of his mouth, the musky smell of him, cologne mingling with sweat and sharp sea air.

Adam levered himself over her, easing his hips between her thighs. His fingers found the most intimate part of her, seeking out her secret, sensitive places. Laura bit down hard upon her lip, finding his gentle touch both ecstasy and torment.

When she felt his hardness pressing against her, she opened to him with an eager readiness. Adam inched himself inside her, filling her, beginning to move. So slowly.

She saw the flush of passion on his face, felt the strain in his tense back muscles, his buttocks as he fought against his culmination.

She sensed him holding back for her sake. Wild, wanton urges seized Laura, such as she'd never known, to test the limits of her feminine power, to drive Adam beyond the brink of his control.

Like cresting waves, she raised up, undulating her hips against him, her body urging him on to a faster, fiercer rhythm. She saw his eyes darken, wintry gray becoming storm-ridden sky. When a hoarse groan breached his lips, she felt a thrill of triumph.

The soft, distant rush of the sea, the coarse feel of the blanket beneath her, the wind-rippled canvas above her head, all became a blur. There was nothing left in her world but Adam, the hard, heated feel of him, the primal joining of their bodies, the hot breath with which he whispered in her ear.

Matching each powerful thrust of his body, her desire built to a frenzy until it shattered in sweet release. A rush of warmth spread through her. She clung to Adam, hearing his guttural cry, the shudder that racked his frame as he reached his own climax.

Panting, he eased his weight from her and tumbled to his back, taking Laura with him. He cradled her against the hard, smooth muscle of his chest, burying his hands in her hair. As her pulse slowed to a normal rate, Laura lay quiet in his arms, fearing one movement, one breath might destroy the wonder of what had just happened.

She wanted to hold fast to this moment, keep it clear in her memory forever, the sound of Adam's strong, steady heartbeat, the gentle brush of his lips against her hair, the far-off melancholy rhythm of the sea.

For so long she had heard Chelsey talk of the joy of sex, the pleasures she found in bed, but it was something Laura had never experienced with Tom Carruthers. Laura had figured Chelsey must be exaggerating. Now Laura knew she hadn't been.

Maybe the difference this time was she hadn't just had sex with Adam Barnhart.

He had made love to her....

"It was wonderful," she murmured, the thought escaping her before she could help it. "Thank you."

"You're welcome." A deep chuckle rumbled in Adam's chest. "The pleasure was all mine, ma'am," he drawled.

Turning, he eased her off his chest to lay beside him, stroking back her hair to peer into her face, his own eyes warm with tender amusement.

"Tell me something," he said. "Are you always this polite in bed?"

"We're not in bed," she reminded him, skating her fingertips up the smooth, taut wall of his chest. "We're in a tent, lost in some faraway desert."

If only it were faraway enough. Laura sighed, aware that the minutes until Chelsey's return were ticking relentlessly away. How could she help but be aware? Laura grimaced, realizing she had made love to Adam with her watch still on.

Adam apparently noticed her glance toward the timepiece for he quirked one brow at her. "Do you have some pressing appointment, Miss Stuart?" he asked. "Perhaps to go see a man about a camel?"

"Er—ah, no." Laura wrenched the watch off her wrist and flung it onto the heap of her discarded clothing. Fears, doubts, feelings of guilt niggled at her, but she firmly shut them out. Nestling close in Adam's arms, she was determined to cling to the afterglow of their lovemaking, bask in this happiness for as long as she could before grim reality intruded.

Adam's fingers skimmed over her waist, her hip, the swell of her thigh, in obvious enjoyment of her soft, feminine curves. In turn, she explored the lean contours of his face, that stubborn granite jaw, the heavy line of his brows, the sensitive curve of his mouth.

His lips twitched into a slight smile beneath her touch. "You've gone kind of quiet all of a sudden. Having regrets?" he whispered.

Laura shook her head to reassure him. At least no regrets about what had just happened between them. Her regrets went much further back than that—to the moment she had first agreed to take part in Chelsey's insane masquerade. If only she had met Adam under normal circumstances, as herself, Laura Stuart. But no, she thought sadly, he would never have looked twice at her.

She forced a smile to her lips, a lighter tone into her voice. "Actually, I was doing some serious considering. About whether you'd make a better sheikh or a pirate. I still have to favor the pirate." She cupped his chin, brushing her thumb over the jagged line that stood out against his deep tan. "You've even got the scar. Acquired fending off some rival buccaneer's saber, no doubt." He caught her hand, pressing a kiss into the center of her palm, sending a pleasant, languorous heat rushing through her. "Actually, the scar is from a crash."

"A crash?" she teased. "Not in your mother's little James Bond car, I hope?"

"No, a plane wreck."

"My God, you were born under a lucky star. Not too many people can boast of walking away from an accident like that."

Something in Adam's eyes seemed to go still. "Yes, I know."

Laura cursed herself. How could she have been so stupid? His brother had died in a plane crash. Then horrified realization slowly dawned on her.

"Oh, Adam, you were with Jack when—when he—"

"When he died? Yes, I was," Adam said flatly.

"I—I'm sorry. I didn't know."

"How could you? It's not something I like to talk about." After a pause, he added, "But I wouldn't mind telling you."

He'd shared the pleasures of lovemaking with her. Now he was willing to share with her his most private pain. He had come to trust her enough even for that and Laura knew with a man like Adam, such trust didn't come easy. She should have been flattered, touched. And she was. She had also never felt lower in her life.

His arms tightened around her as he explained, "Jack was crazy for anything that had a motor. He'd just gotten his pilot's license and he was thinking of expanding Barnhart Shipping to include the manufacture of seaplanes. He had this new model he wanted to test and asked me if I wanted to go up with him."

Adam gave a sad kind of laugh. "Hell, I've never liked flying that much, but I'd have gone on a rocket ship to the moon if Jack had been the captain. He was a good pilot. He was good at everything. I'm still not sure what went wrong.

"One minute he was kidding me about needing an air-sick bag and the next he was swearing at the control panel. We went plummeting down toward the shore like some crazed roller coaster jumping its tracks."

Adam closed his eyes for a moment before continuing. "We crash-landed on an empty stretch of beach, not five miles from here. Somehow I came out of it with a broken leg, some cracked ribs and this." Adam rubbed the scar on his chin and swallowed. "But Jack... he didn't even make it to the hospital."

Laura felt a thickness gather in her own throat. She wrapped her arms about Adam's neck, wanting to offer some great words of wisdom, of comfort. But all she could get out was, "Oh, Adam. I'm so sorry."

She felt the movement of his shoulders as he tried to shrug. "It was just one of those freak things, I guess, those quirks of fate that don't make sense. Why should I have survived and not Jack? The father of two kids, the driving force behind our family business, so important to so many people."

"So were you," Laura cried.

But Adam only shook his head. "Part of me knows it's not logical. The accident certainly wasn't my fault. But another part of me can't help feeling... guilty."

Laura raised herself up on one elbow, smoothing her fingers over the furrows on Adam's troubled brow. "I'm sure your brother would never have wanted that. Jack would have to be grateful for all you've done for his children, his business." She hesitated before adding gently, "But, Adam,

I don't think he would have expected you to live out the rest of his life for him."

Adam frowned, and Laura feared perhaps she'd said too much. But then he sighed and said slowly, "You're right, but the truth is I haven't cared too much about my own life. Until recently."

"You mean, until you started getting interested in architecture again, until you started trying to save the old house."

"No," he said huskily. "I meant until I met you."

The look in his eyes was so earnest, so tender, Laura felt her heart swell with an ache that was nearly unbearable, her emotions at hearing him confess such a thing painfully bittersweet.

With a low groan, Laura rolled away from him, burying her face in her hands.

"Chelsey?" Laura heard the anxious note in Adam's voice. His hand settled warmly on her shoulder. "Did I say something wrong?"

No, it wasn't what he had said. It was what she hadn't.

"Adam, you don't know...you don't understand. I don't deserve—" Laura choked, a hot tear escaping down her cheek. She was unable to continue.

"Yes, you do," he insisted. "Chelsey, you'll never know what being with you these past few days has done for me. I feel like a different man. We hardly know each other, and yet when I'm with you I feel as if it's been forever. I feel—"

"Oh, Adam. Don't! Please," she cried. Why didn't he just stab her through the heart and be done with it? She'd been waiting a lifetime to hear someone like Adam tell her such things, how wonderful and special she was to him, and yet she couldn't let him go on. Not when she continued to deceive him this way.

She sensed his puzzlement and his hurt. But before she could swallow her tears enough to speak, he gave an uneasy laugh. "I'm sorry, Chelsey. I didn't mean to alarm you by getting so serious all of a sudden."

"No, Adam. It—it's all my fault. I—"

"Don't be ridiculous," he said, gathering her back into his arms despite her feeble effort at resistance. "It's okay. I understand. It's me who was rushing things, and we don't have to." He pressed his lips to her hair, her brow, kissing away the remnants of a tear that stained her cheek. "We have all the time in the world to get to know each other better."

No, they didn't. Laura suppressed a deep shudder and buried her face helplessly against the strong comfort of Adam's shoulder. Even above the rush of the sea, the hammering of her own heart, she thought she could hear the remorseless ticking of her watch.

Chelsey's twelve hours were almost over.

And so were hers.

Nine

She couldn't tell him.

Adam had made love to her again. Afterward they had dressed and sat on the beach, watching the sun go down and the moon rise, spilling its shimmering light across a tranquil sea.

And still Laura could not seem to find the words to tell Adam the truth.

As they trudged back to the beach house, Adam's arm wrapped lightly about her shoulders, Laura experienced a sense of mounting panic. She couldn't fool herself any longer. Her continuing silence had nothing to do with the promise she'd made to her sister. She'd had dozens of reasonable opportunities this afternoon in which she could have confessed to Adam and done Chelsey no harm.

But Laura had availed herself of none of them. The plain fact was that she was scared, scared of what Adam's reaction would be. With a sense of the most wretched irony, she recalled her blithe advice to Chelsey.

Just tell Luke the truth. If he really loves you, he'll understand.

Chelsey's bitter reply seemed to come back to haunt her now, drifting on the evening breeze.

You always think everything's so simple, Laura.

Laura supposed that Chelsey was right. She had a habit of seeing everything in black-and-white, no shades of gray. But perhaps that was because Laura had never found herself falling in love before. And being in love could suddenly make everything very complicated.

But complicated or not, Laura knew she had to do something fast. She and Adam were nearly back at the beach house and she could see a light shining from the upper level. It might only be Adam's mother returned from her golf game and dinner engagement.

But it was after nine o'clock and it might just as well be Chelsey and Luke. A Luke who now knew the truth, by Laura's own insistence. Why, oh, why, Laura thought with an inward groan, had she been so tough on Chelsey? Having taken the charade this far, she thought wistfully, was there any reason it couldn't have gone on a little longer? The rest of the weekend, perhaps.

And maybe you and Chelsey could have just found some way to switch birth certificates, an acid voice echoed inside Laura's head. Tell Adam the truth, you idiot. Now!

Laura knew the voice was right. She was being ridiculous. As he guided her along the flagstone pathway that led to the beachside doors on the lower level, Laura drew in a deep breath and came to an abrupt halt.

"Adam..."

"Yes?"

She shivered and he must have thought she was cold, for he wrapped his arm tighter about her, the feel of his callused palm against her skin warm and reassuring. The light shining from the house illuminated the hard, chiseled contours of his profile, his dark gray eyes reflecting the same fire and brilliance as the stars in the overhead sky.

Oh, God, Laura thought. Did he have to glance down at her in that way, which melted her to the marrow of her bones?

Tell him, the merciless voice prodded.

Laura moistened her lips. But she just couldn't come out with such a daunting confession in a blunt fashion. There had to be some way of easing into this. Her mind worked feverishly, until at last she blurted out, "Have you ever read any fairy tales?"

"What?" Adam stared at her as if uncertain he'd heard her correctly.

"You know, fairy tales. Like Cinderella."

"I guess I'm familiar with the story."

"You remember the part where the prince finds Cinderella with the glass slipper?"

"Ye-e-ss," Adam said slowly. He looked nonplussed by the conversation but willing to humor her.

"And everything turned out fine because the prince loved her. But he could have been very upset with Cinderella, couldn't he?"

"I don't know. Could he?"

"Yes, he could!" Laura said, becoming distressed because she had a feeling that Adam wasn't following her at all. "And he would've had a right to be upset. After all, he thought Cinderella was this glamorous, sexy princess, only to find out she was nothing but—but a meek sort of cleaning lady."

Adam laughed. "It's only a fairy tale, Chelsey. I never thought they got that complex, but then as I said, I never read them much."

He brushed a light kiss on the tip of her nose. "You know what?" he murmured. "I think you're getting light-headed for lack of food. It occurs to me we skipped dinner, and I'm starving. Come on."

He tugged her toward the house, and although Laura tried to hang back, he started to undo the latch on the sliding glass doors.

"Adam, wait!" Laura cried desperately. "This is really important."

He paused to glance back at her.

Laura fretted her lip and tried again. "Did you ever read *The Prince and the Pauper* by Mark Twain?"

At Adam's blank expression, she rushed on, "You know, the story about the two boys who switched places."

Adam regarded her warily, as if he were beginning to doubt her sanity. "No, I can't say as I'm very familiar with that story, either."

"What in the world did you read when you were a little boy?" Laura demanded, torn between misery and exasperation.

"Architectural Digest." Adam slid open the glass door and paused on the threshold, his smile fading. "I'm beginning to get the strangest feeling you're trying to tell me something, Chelsey. May I recommend a more direct approach? I find that's always best."

So did she, Laura thought. Under normal circumstances. But these were far from normal circumstances. As Adam reached inside the house, groping for a light switch, Laura took a deep breath. Blinking against the sudden flood of illumination, she said, "The truth is, I'm not Chelsey. I'm Laura."

"Sonofabitch! What the hell!"

Laura flinched. She'd been afraid Adam wouldn't take it well, but she hadn't expect this violent a response. But when she dared to glance up, she realized that it wasn't her Adam was swearing at, but something he saw in the house. He probably hadn't even heard her whispered confession. As he strode through the sliding doors, vanishing into the house, Laura's shoulders sagged. Now she was going to have to work up her nerve all over again.

Following him inside, she doubted whatever calamity waited inside could surpass her own predicament.

She was wrong. She was as alarmed as Adam by the sight that met her eyes. The lower level of the Barnhart beach house had been converted into a rec room. But just beyond the pool table was a small alcove that Adam used for an office.

Through the open door, Laura could see Adam wading through what looked like the remains of an earthquake. Desk drawers and file cabinets had all been turned topsy-turvy, papers and folders littered everywhere. Even books had been dragged off the shelf and dumped on the floor.

"My God," Laura murmured. She trailed Adam as far as the room's threshold. "Adam?" she called uncertainly.

He seemed to have gone a little crazy. His face a hard mask of fury and disbelief, he hunkered down, shoving aside architectural textbooks, tearing through piles of canceled checks, typing paper and legal forms as if in frantic search of something.

As her initial shock wore off, comprehension of the chaos before her settled in and the back of her neck prickled. While she and Adam had made love only yards away down the beach, the house had been broken into. Laura stole a nervous glance around, half expecting to find some hooded menace creeping up on them.

From beneath the desk, Adam dragged out a small fireproof box that had been discarded on its side. It was dented, as if it had been smashed open. The lid came half off the hinges as Adam checked inside. Empty.

Adam didn't look as much surprised as sickened, infuriated. Straightening to his feet, he flung the box down with a force and savage oath that made Laura jump.

"Adam," she said. "What—what's wrong? What's missing?"

Adam jammed his fingers back through his hair in a gesture of pure frustration. "Only all the deeds and documents I had on the house in Belle's Point."

Laura's own heart turned over with sick despair. "Oh, Adam. Not the ones you were going to use in court to fight Storm?"

Adam nodded grimly. "That bastard! Who'd have ever thought he'd go this far? And how the hell did he even know I had those deeds?"

"You think Storm did this?"

"Who else?"

"Somehow I can't picture Storm rifling through your office in his Savile Row suit."

"So he hired someone else to do his dirty work and keep him in the clear like he always does. What the hell difference does it make?" Adam sagged down in the swivel chair behind the desk, the green leather creaking beneath his weight. "Either way, Storm's got the papers by now."

"But shouldn't we call the police?"

"What for? How would I prove anything? The first thing Storm will do is set a match to those deeds."

"You don't know that. It might be possible to still catch the thief."

"I'm sure whoever's been here is long gone and was damned careful not to leave any trace—"

A loud crash sounded from the regions up above, cutting off Adam in midsentence. Laura and Adam exchanged startled glances. They both tensed, listening. A footfall sounded. Someone was creeping down the stairs to the lower level.

Adam came up out of his chair and crossed the room in two stealthy strides. Shoving Laura behind him into the vicinity of the office, he whispered tersely, "Stay here."

"Adam, no!" Laura said back. She clung to his arm, alarmed by visions of Adam being knocked unconscious, shot or even worse by whatever thug might be closing in.

Before Adam could argue or thrust her away, a voice called out, "Who's down here?"

Chelsey.

Laura almost sagged against Adam with relief. Then she immediately stiffened. Chelsey! In her distress over the break-in, Laura had forgotten her more immediate problem.

She brushed past Adam, hoping to intercept her sister, but it was already too late. Chelsey appeared in the office doorway.

"Oh, it's only you two. I wondered when anybody else would turn up around here."

Any doubts Laura had had as to whether Chelsey had kept her promise and ended the masquerade were dispelled by the sight of her sister. Chelsey had poured herself back into a pair of her own tight jeans, a tight-fitting black knit top pulled down to bare her shoulders.

She also appeared to have poured herself a large whiskey, a half-empty glass of the amber liquid still clutched in her hand. Her eyes skimmed over the disaster in Adam's office, and she said, "Geez, Barnhart, you're even messier than I am."

Adam frowned, obviously taken aback by this abrupt change in the woman he had come to regard as the circumspect L.C. Stuart. Laura knew she had to get Chelsey out of there fast. She recognized the danger signals in Chelsey's face, the hard brilliance of the eyes, the chip-on-the-shoulder attitude Chelsey always adopted when she was upset about something. Whatever had taken place between Chelsey and Luke could not have been pleasant.

Laura laid her hand on Chelsey's arm, trying to telegraph a warning with her eyes. "We're having a bit of a problem here, *L.C.!* If you could just go back upstairs with Luke..."

"You can drop the L.C. bit." Chelsey took another gulp of the whiskey and pulled a sour face. "You gave me a twelve-hour ultimatum, remember? And Luke's not here. He went off to drown his sorrows in the wild nightlife of Belle's Point. He wasn't too keen for my company just now. Or ever."

"You and Luke had a falling out?" Adam scowled.

"Yeah, that must make your day, Barnhart. You finally got what you wanted. When I told Luke the truth, he acted like I drowned his puppy."

"The truth? The truth about what?"

"L.C., please!" Laura whispered, trying to thrust her sister out of the room. But Chelsey refused to budge.

She stared at Laura reproachfully. "You haven't told Adam yet, have you?"

"Told me what?" Adam demanded with rising impatience.

"I—I was just getting around to it..." Laura faltered.

"Oh, that's classic." Chelsey waved her hand in a wild arc, nearly spilling the rest of her drink. "You force me into telling Luke and now you're the one who's stalling."

Adam's gaze skipped from Laura to Chelsey, then back again, his eyes narrowing. "Just what the hell is going on here?"

"Do you want to explain, Miss Truth or Consequences?" Chelsey asked bitterly. "Or shall I?"

"I'll do it," Laura said, although she could feel her throat closing up. If there'd ever been a night when she needed her inhaler again, she feared this was going to be it. She thought turning to face Adam was the most difficult thing she'd ever done in her life.

"It's what I was trying to tell you earlier, Adam," Laura began.

"What? You mean all the nonsense about Cinderella and the pauper?"

"Yes. That is, no! What I was really attempting to say is—" Laura gestured helplessly toward Chelsey. "I'm not me. And she isn't her."

"That really clarifies everything," Chelsey muttered.

Laura rounded on her sister. "Will you please stay out of this! Could you just leave Adam and me alone for a while?"

"I would've thought you had plenty of time for that," Chelsey said with acid sweetness. When Laura glared at her, she shrugged. "All right, I'm going. I wish you better luck with your explanations than I had."

Better luck? That wasn't likely. As Chelsey ambled back upstairs to the living room, Laura stole a glance at Adam's face. He had crossed his arms over his chest, his expression far from encouraging.

Laura took another fortifying breath. "The truth is, Adam, that—that Chelsey and I..."

As she stumbled for words, Adam cut in harshly, "Never mind. I may be a little dense, but I think I'm finally getting the drift. You and your sister switched places."

Laura nodded unhappily.

Adam thought he couldn't have been more stunned if she had brought the roof crashing down on his head. He'd always been thrown a little off balance by the woman he'd believed to be Chelsey Stuart, always sensed something was not quite right. But to ever imagine two fully grown women could be capable of changing identities like a pair of incorrigible kids... It was fantastic. It was incredible.

Brushing past Laura, Adam paced into the rec room, rubbing the back of his neck, trying to absorb the full impact of what she'd just told him. His thoughts flashed back over the weekend, a dozen inconsistencies that now made sense, her almost drowning in the pool, the peculiar way she had acted around Storm, how she had fumbled with the camera this afternoon.

This afternoon . . . Adam grimaced, his mind filling with other images far more intimate and tender, images of how he'd held her in his arms, made love to her, shared ambitions, dreams, griefs that he'd kept locked away for years, bared himself, both body and soul. He, who prided himself on being so hardheaded and practical, had almost succumbed to the biggest romantic myth of all time, the belief in love at first sight, kindred spirits finding each other. Even on such short acquaintance he had convinced himself that he knew this woman, really *knew* her.

The irony of that now struck him full force and he felt seven kinds of a fool.

"Adam?"

She had trailed after him. Kneading her fingers together, she watched him with anxious eyes. "Please," she said. "Shout at me, swear at me, but say *something.*"

"What's there to say? Congratulations? You and your sister managed to pull off one helluva practical joke."

"It wasn't a joke. Chelsey and I had a reason for what we did."

"A good reason for this lunacy? I'm dying to hear it."

"I didn't say it was a good reason," she said in a small voice. "Just a reason."

"I can't imagine what possible—" He broke off, comprehension dawning on him like a swift blow to the head. "Of course, Luke. I *am* a fool. This really was all a ploy for your sister to get her hooks into Luke."

"She loves him," Laura protested, "But, yes, Chelsey knew you already disapproved of their relationship. She thought by pretending to be me, you might find her more acceptable. But then I turned up when she didn't expect me."

"And you just went along to help out. How noble of you."

"It wasn't noble at all." She hung her head. "It was stupid. I never should have... I just never thought that things would go this far."

"I'll bet you didn't. You must have had some real awkward moments this weekend. So you don't photograph naked men? You're the artistic one. What do you use, your sketch pad?"

"I don't draw men at all." She made a wan attempt to smile. "Just rabbits."

"Maybe you should take up acting, instead. You seem to have a real talent for it. That was quite a performance you gave that night by the pool... at least, I think that was you I was kissing that night."

"Of course it was," Laura said indignantly.

"Excuse me for being confused. It could have been your sister. I'm not quite sure how I'm supposed to tell the difference between you."

She flinched under his sarcasm. "Please don't, Adam. I feel awful enough already."

But Adam was experiencing the first stings of anger, wounded pride mixing with a sense of raw hurt. "So what the hell am I supposed to call you now? L.C.?"

"Laura. Just plain Laura."

"Laura," he repeated, the sound of it somehow so gentle, it only added to his feelings of betrayal. "It might have been nice to have known that on the beach this afternoon. Call me old-fashioned, but I always like to know the real name of a woman when I'm making love to her."

"I wanted to tell you, Adam."

"Then why didn't you?" he snapped.

"You kept kissing me. I—I couldn't think."

"I must have let you come up for air sometime."

"I was afraid."

"What did you think I'd do? Punch you for lying to me?"

"No. I was afraid you...you wouldn't still want me." She gazed up at him, her eyes large and wistful.

Not want her? That was the hell of it. Despite the deception she'd practiced, he still wanted her, wanted to pull Laura into his arms, tell her he understood. Tell her it was all right. And the desire only added fuel to his anger.

Because, damn it, it wasn't all right!

"I'm nothing like what I pretended to be," she continued. "Chelsey's the daring one, the sexy one. I never have romantic escapades or adventures."

"I sure hope you enjoyed this one," Adam said bitterly.

Laura glanced up at him, dismayed. "Adam, you can't possibly think that what happened between us meant no more to me than that."

He didn't answer her, but he didn't have to. She could tell from the look in his eyes, that's exactly what he thought. She rested her hand pleadingly against the unyielding wall of his chest, stumbling over words in her effort to reassure him. But she had a sinking feeling it didn't matter. Adam didn't seem inclined to believe anything she might have to say, and she couldn't blame him.

The phone rang, the jangling sound only adding to the tension that pulsed between her and Adam. He ignored it for a moment, then with an oath turned aside to answer it.

"Barnhart here," he snapped into the receiver. There was a pause, and then he said slowly, "Yes, I do have a nephew named Luke. What's wrong?"

He lapsed into silence, looking more grim by the moment, as the voice at the other end crackled in his ear. Laura's stomach clenched with alarm as she waited for Adam to finish.

"I see," he said at last. "I'll be right there."

As he hung up the phone, Laura cried. "Adam, what is it? What's happened?"

"That was a bartender in Belle's Point. It seems Luke's drunk on his butt. He can't even stand, but he's trying to leave. They've taken his car keys away from him. I'm going to have to go get him before he ends up in jail."

Adam headed for the stairs, and Laura hurried after him. She had thought this disaster couldn't get any worse. It seems she had been wrong.

"Adam, I'm so sorry." The words sounded inadequate, even to her. Laura couldn't remember feeling more wretched, more guilty, not since the time she had believed herself responsible for her parents' divorce.

"You ought to be sorry." Adam paused on the step above her. "You're the one who kept telling me Luke wasn't going to be hurt by your sister."

"I—I know. Let me come with you, Adam. Maybe I can help you with Luke—"

"No, thanks. You and your sister have both done quite enough."

"It's a poor excuse, I know, but Chelsey didn't mean to hurt Luke . . . any more than I meant to hurt you."

Laura rested her hand on his sleeve. He didn't seek to evade her touch so much as ignore it, his muscles tense and unforgiving beneath her fingertips.

"I'll survive," he said. "I'm not a shy, sensitive kid like Luke. I'm just a man who should've known better than to indulge in a fling with a woman I just met."

"A fling?" she faltered.

"An adventure, isn't that what you called it?" He regarded her with a jaded weariness that seemed to mock her and himself as well. "But that's the trouble with these little weekend adventures, Laura. They come to an end. And as far as I'm concerned, this one is over."

Bending down, he captured her lips in a kiss that was hard, quick and very final. Before Laura could catch her breath to even protest, he was up the stairs and gone.

Laura stared at the closed door, her eyes stinging with tears.

"It wasn't just an adventure, Adam," she whispered. "I love you."

But like so much else that she had waited to tell him, the confession came far too late.

Ten

Laura's packed suitcase stood by the front door ready to go. She caught a glimpse of herself in the mirror that hung behind the bar in the living room and grimaced. She had never realized it before, but her beige linen suit really did make her look washed out, colorless. Or maybe she was just pale from a sleepless night.

Cinderella, the morning after the ball. Only she had a bleak feeling that Prince Charming wasn't going to turn up with the slipper. There'd been no sign of Adam since he'd left her last night. Maybe he'd just decided to join Luke at that bar, both of them drinking themselves insensible while darkly discussing the perfidy of all women.

Or maybe he'd just avoided coming back to the beach house, not wanting to see her again. Laura sighed. Well, she intended to relieve him of that awkward possibility as soon as she could arrange a ride to the nearest bus station.

She headed for the only part of the house where she heard life stirring, the kitchen. Louise Barnhart stood near the counter. Glasses perched on the rim of her nose, she studied the instructions on a package of microwave pancakes with as much concentration as if she were preparing a gourmet recipe.

But she looked up and beamed. "Good morning... Chelsey, isn't it?"

"No, it's Laura," Laura said, feeling extremely foolish.

"Well, never mind. Eventually I'll get good at telling you girls apart."

"I suppose Chelsey and I haven't helped matters."

But Lou only grinned at her. Adam's mother had taken the news of the deception all in stride. In fact, she had even been faintly amused by it.

Coaxing Laura to come have a cup of instant coffee, she said, "You look as if you were all decked out for church."

"Actually, I'm decked out—I mean, dressed to leave," Laura confessed.

Placing a steaming cup in front of Laura, Lou said, "Oh, no. You can't think of leaving so soon. At least not until Adam gets back."

"He and Luke are still at the bar?"

Louise laughed. "In Belle's Point on a Sunday? Not likely. We have more blue laws here than Ocean City. No, Adam went into town, to the house."

Laura didn't even have to ask what house. After all that had happened, she had nearly forgotten about the break-in, the missing deeds.

"What's Adam doing there so early?" she asked.

"He had some restoration person coming around to give him an opinion about matching that old siding. Adam was going to tell the man not to bother."

"Not to bother!"

"Adam said something about Storm being right about fixing up the house. It was a waste of time."

Laura couldn't imagine how bitter Adam had to be to say a thing like that. Any hope she'd had that he might be feeling differently this morning, swiftly died. Laura shoved her coffee away, untasted.

Louise peered at Laura over the rims of her glasses. The woman could seem flighty at times, but there was a shrewd intelligence to be found lurking in her gray eyes and a great deal of sympathy.

"You shouldn't worry over Adam, dear," she said, giving Laura's shoulder a gentle pat. "I don't know how he reacted when you confessed to him last night, but I imagine he cut up pretty rough. Barnhart men have been known to misplace their sense of humor from time to time. But they always find it again."

Laura forced a smile to her lips, knowing Louise was only trying to be helpful. But she didn't understand. It wasn't his humor Adam had misplaced, but his trust. Laura had shattered it into a thousand bits, and she didn't think there was any way of repairing that damage.

"I don't know," Laura said, slowly shaking her head. "Adam was awfully upset. Especially about Luke."

"Luke's just fine."

"Oh, no, he was devastated."

"He didn't look particularly devastated to me this morning. But maybe you'd better go out back and see for yourself."

Puzzled, Laura did as Louise suggested, letting herself out the back doors and stepping onto the deck.

The sound of laughter drifted up to her from the poolside. Creeping close to the deck rail, she peeked down in the backyard with disbelief. There was Luke in his trunks, stretched out in a deck chair.

He did look a little peaked and was making faces at some fizzling bromide Chelsey was forcing down his throat. But between sips, he was regaling Chelsey with what had happened at the bar last night.

His voice carried up to Laura "And after I got up on top of the bar with this go-go dancer, I think I must've started stripping off my clothes. This redhead in the back got so excited, she damn near had a heart attack."

Chelsey choked on her laughter, nearly dumping the rest of the bromide all over Luke. Laura compressed her lips together. It was obvious her sister had been a sterling influence on Luke. Laura supposed she ought to be glad to see that the two of them had patched things up, but after the misery she and Adam had gone through, she felt a wave of irritation sweep over her.

Marching down the deck stairs, Laura strode across the lawn toward the poolside. Chelsey glanced up and accorded her a causal wave.

"Laura, you're finally up and about. Anyone would think it was you with the hangover, instead of poor Luke."

"Poor Luke looks just fine to me," Laura said tartly.

"I'm feeling better now. L.C.—I mean, Chelsey makes a real sexy nurse." He tried to slip his arm about Chelsey's waist, and she slapped his hand playfully away.

"You better drink up the rest of this bromide or you'll be calling me Nurse Ratchett."

As Laura watched this bit of byplay, she felt her blood pressure bump up another notch.

"Your uncle was worried sick about you last night," Laura told him.

Luke shrugged and then winced pressing his hand to his temple. "He shouldn't have been. I'm over twenty-one."

"Then why don't you act like it?" Laura asked sweetly.

Luke gaped at her.

"Lighten up, Laura," Chelsey said. "Everything's fine now."

"Sure," Luke agreed. "I admit it gave me a jolt when Chelsey first told me the truth. But looking back, the whole thing seems kind of funny."

"Oh, yes, it's all real amusing," Laura said through clenched teeth. "So you two just kissed and made up."

Luke and Chelsey exchanged a sheepish glance. "Well, not exactly," Luke said.

"What do you mean, not exactly?"

"We-elll," Chelsey drawled. "Luke and I decided to cool things down a bit. Just be friends for a while."

"Friends?" Laura echoed.

"It's the damnedest thing." Chelsey looked a little embarrassed. "Actually, the funniest part of this whole business. You're going to laugh when I tell you this, Laura. Luke and I realized we're not in love with each other, after all."

Chelsey flashed her a brilliant smile and chuckled a little. But Laura didn't feel in the least like laughing. Her sister had always had a habit of stretching the patience of people, just like tugging on a giant rubber band.

And Laura felt something deep inside herself go snap.

"Not in love?" she repeated in a strangled tone.

"Yeah, it's a good thing we figured that out, huh?" Chelsey grinned. But her smile wavered as Laura stalked closer. "Laura? You okay? You've got a real strange look in your eyes. Laura!" Chelsey's voice rose on a startled cry as Laura pounced.

She grabbed Chelsey's arm. Wrenching it behind Chelsey's back, Laura propelled her toward the edge of the pool. Her sister was too stunned to offer much resistance.

"What the hell are you—" Chelsey's sputterings ended in a shriek and loud splash as Laura shoved her into the deep end of the pool.

Laura felt no qualms about the violence of her actions. In fact, she couldn't remember when anything had given her so much satisfaction. She whipped about to find Luke struggling up from his deck chair.

"Chelsey!" He staggered forward as if prepared to dive to the rescue. But Laura blocked his path.

"Don't worry about her. She's the world's champion swimmer. She always comes out on top."

Luke backed away from Laura, looking as if he doubted her sanity.

Laura pursued him, saying, "You are going to go into the house and get dressed."

"I—I—yes, ma'am." Under other circumstances, Luke's retreat from her would have been almost comical.

But Laura maintained her fierce demeanor. "Then you are going to drive me to the bus depot."

"Yes, ma'am."

Behind her, Laura heard Chelsey coughing and panting as she struggled up the ladder out of the pool. "Laura! You're behaving like a lunatic. Where are you going?"

Laura hadn't been certain before. But suddenly she knew. Maybe it was the adrenaline still pumping through her veins. Perhaps there was no way of making up to Adam for the deception she had practiced, but there was one thing she might be able to do for him.

"I'm going to Atlantic City," Laura announced, setting her jaw in a hard, determined line. "To see a man about some deeds to a house."

Laura's courage didn't fail her until she actually stood outside the imposing double doors that led to Xavier Storm's penthouse suite. She'd had too much time to think on the bus ride to Atlantic City and through the long minutes of getting past Storm's fortresslike security system.

The man lived high atop his own multimillion-dollar hotel and casino set in isolation at the far end of the boardwalk. He had a host of guards who could have rivaled the

Secret Service, but at the mention of her name Laura found herself miraculously escorted past each checkpoint.

Which was strange because she didn't think Storm even knew that Laura Stuart existed, unless Chelsey had ever talked about her sister. The trip up in the private elevator alone would have been enough to make one uneasy, the whole experience of penetrating deeper into Storm's bastion calculated to impress one with the man's wealth and power.

She must have been out of her mind to come here. She had no proof Storm was behind the break-in, only hers and Adam's gut-level instincts. How in the world was she going to get a man as suave and ruthless as Storm to confess?

But she had come too far to back down now. Jabbing at the door buzzer, Laura clutched her purse in front of her and waited. Some moments later one of the double doors eased open.

Laura expected to be greeted by some supercilious white-jacketed valet or houseboy, the kind one saw in old movies. Her breath snagged in her throat when Storm himself appeared, lounging in the doorway.

It was late afternoon, but the man was still clad only in his black satin bathrobe and—Laura stole a nervous glance at the glimpse of bare chest, bare legs—she feared he wore nothing beneath.

His black hair was mussed, his lean jaw unshaven. He was the image of every wealthy playboy, every wicked seducer who Laura had ever read about. He regarded her for a moment through those unnerving, hooded eyes, then drawled, "Well, come in."

Said the spider to the fly.

Laura took a deep breath and stepped across the threshold. "You don't know me, Mr. Storm," she began primly.

"Yes, I do. It's Laura, isn't it? Chelsey's sister." A faint, mocking smile creased his lips.

"Yes." Laura gasped and caught herself as she nearly stumbled down the step into the penthouse's sunken living room. All white, black and chrome, the place was stark, the furnishings holding all the personality of a hotel suite. Curtains were drawn back to reveal a wall of windows, overlooking, at a lordly distance, the stretch of boardwalk with its glitzy array of hotels and casinos, the gray Atlantic leaving wet tracings along the shoreline.

The coffee table and sofa were littered with sections of the morning paper, an empty mug and a half-eaten box of doughnuts. It made for a strange contrast, reminding Laura curiously of long-ago Sundays spent with her family at home. But Storm was all alone.

Closing the front door, he sauntered past her, saying, "Sit down. Can I get you anything? Coffee? Jelly doughnut?"

"No, thank you." Storm wasn't the sort of man any self-respecting woman should accept sweets from. And besides that, her stomach was tied up in knots.

He shoved aside the comics section and sank down on a white love seat, lounging back against the cushions. "Did you bring the pictures?"

"What pictures?" Laura asked, then memory rushed through her. The pictures for *She* magazine, that's what Storm was talking about. So what she'd suspected yesterday was true. Storm had been entertaining himself at her expense. A hot flood of color surged into Laura's cheeks.

"You knew all along, didn't you?" she said indignantly. "When you came to Belle's Point yesterday, you realized I wasn't Chelsey."

"It didn't require a great amount of perception. I knew Chelsey had a twin."

"But—but how could you tell so fast?"

Storm shrugged. "I've never seen your sister blush. And no one has ever called me 'Xavier' or 'hon.' It was a unique experience."

"But Adam never guessed," Laura murmured sadly.

"Ah, but then I didn't look at you in the same way as your crusading boat builder does."

"Architect," Laura corrected.

"Whatever." Storm shuddered. "I can only say thank God I've never been that besotted about any woman."

Adam besotted about her? Storm wasn't quite as perceptive as he flattered himself to be. But Laura let the man's comment pass.

"So I'm dying to see the pictures. Did you bring them?" Storm asked.

"No! I've come on quite a different matter." Steeling her nerve, she said, "I have reason to believe you've come into possession of something that belongs to Adam Barnhart."

"Have I? That can hardly be called my fault. I didn't invite you here."

"I'm not talking about me," Laura choked. "I mean certain documents."

"Documents?" Storm arched one slender black eyebrow.

"Regarding the old house on your property in Belle's Point?" Laura spoke as firmly as she could for one so unsure of her ground. What if she was wrong? What if Storm had had nothing to do with the robbery? But a secretive amusement clung to his lips, his narrowed eyes too full of the devil for the man to be innocent.

She would browbeat him into confessing if she had to, though she scarcely knew how. But she had seen enough episodes of "Perry Mason," watched the stocky lawyer hammering away at some guilty witness until they broke down and admitted the truth.

"Mr. Storm," she said. "Adam's beach house was broken into last night. Documents disappeared that could have helped him win his court case against you. Documents that only you—"

"Those ridiculous pieces of ancient parchment? They're over there." Storm indicated a glass end table with a careless gesture.

Laura blinked. Not even Perry had ever obtained results that fast. Storm's brazen confession threw her off balance, left her feeling almost deflated. She had braced herself for a fight. Surely it couldn't be this easy.

She moved cautiously to the end table and picked up the manila envelope she found there. A quick examination revealed the contents to be Adam's missing papers. A sigh of relief escaped her. So Storm hadn't destroyed them yet, as Adam had feared he would do.

But her relief was short-lived. Laura started as Storm's hand suddenly shot out and plucked the papers from her. The man could move with the silence of a stalking panther. She turned, finding him standing uncomfortably close, so close she could smell the musky, expensive scent of his cologne.

"Mr. Storm, I don't know how you gained possession of these papers but—"

"A rather distasteful youth named Leaming brought them to me this morning, demanding an exorbitant sum."

Chad Leaming. Of course, Laura thought with a groan. Why hadn't she thought of him sooner? Working at the Barnharts', he would have had plenty of opportunity to overhear about the documents, figure out their value to a wealthy man like Storm.

"I don't care what you paid to get them," Laura cried, "those papers don't belong to you." She made a grab for them, but Storm held them easily out of her reach.

"What's your interest in all this, I wonder?" he taunted. "You thinking of setting up housekeeping with Mr. Barnhart? Surely your boat builder can do better by you than that tumbledown wreck of a house?"

"I told you he's not a boat builder. He's an architect. A fine one, and full of more dreams and ideals than a person like you could ever understand."

"I probably couldn't," Storm agreed affably.

"And if you don't give me those papers, I'll call the police."

"You mean you didn't think to alert the police before you came? You just came barging up here all alone?" Storm's smile sent a sudden chill through Laura. "But how foolish of you," he purred.

Her heart gave an uneasy thud. "I—I'm not afraid of you."

"You're not?" he asked softly, moving relentlessly closer. "You should be. Most people are."

"Keep back! I'm warning you, Storm. I—I have a knee and I know how to use it."

The threat sounded so ridiculous, Laura grimaced herself. But to her astonishment, Storm stopped cold in his tracks. He laughed, not his usual mockery, but a sound of genuine amusement.

Then he seized her hand. Before Laura could even gasp, he slapped the documents into her open palm. Laura stared down at the papers, uncomprehending.

"You don't really think I have any interest in those ridiculous documents, do you?" he demanded.

"But—but the court case with Adam. You want to win, don't you?"

"Oh, I'll win. I always do. But on my own terms. If I was going to mastermind a break-in, I wouldn't hire a young hoodlum who suffers from acne."

"But you paid Chad Leaming—"

"No, I only said he asked for money. Actually, I relieved him of the documents and had him escorted—er—gently from the premises."

"Then you meant to return the papers to Adam all along?" Laura asked incredulously.

Storm's lips curled into a half smile. "I wouldn't go so far as to say that. That would depend entirely on my mood. But since you came and asked so charmingly, how could I resist?"

Laura felt her cheeks heat. "I'm sorry if I was rude, accusing you of something you didn't do."

"I'm accustomed to that," Storm said dryly. "Didn't you know I'm responsible for everything from the poor economy to the depletion of the ozone layer?"

Laura couldn't tell from his tone if he was mocking himself or her.

"You're a very... strange man, Mr. Storm," she murmured.

"And you're an intriguing woman, Miss Stuart. Even more so than your sister. Someday I'd love to hear the story of what you were up to, impersonating Chelsey. If you ever get tired of your crusading architect, why don't you give me a call?" He produced a card, which he held out to her.

But Laura backed away warily, shaking her head. "I—I don't think so, Mr. Storm. I've already been enough out of my league this weekend."

Storm returned the card to its gold case, not appearing offended by her refusal or even particularly interested.

"I'd better be going," Laura said, retreating toward the door. "I've taken up enough of your valuable time."

"Oh, yes, my valuable time. There's always more corporations to raid, mortgages to foreclose. I trust you can see yourself out?"

Laura nodded. In fact, she was thinking of making a bolt for it before he changed his mind about letting her have the deeds. But Storm had already stridden away, like an emperor dismissing his audience.

As Laura turned the handle of the door, her last impression was of him standing by the windows, a stark, lonely figure looking out over his distant empire.

Once on the other side of the door, Laura hastened toward the elevator. She jabbed the button and leaned up against the wall, feeling almost weak with relief, feeling a curious sense of elation as well.

She'd confronted Storm, gotten Adam's papers back and she wasn't even breathing hard. She no longer felt the need to go groping through her purse, seeking the comfort of her inhaler just in case. That childhood terror finally seemed behind her. In fact... Laura pawed through her purse, found the inhaler and dropped it in the small metal ashcan next to the elevator.

And now to get the deeds back to Adam. Perhaps when he saw what she had done, he would...

Would what? Fall at her feet in a fit of gratitude? Decide to forgive her? No. Her shoulders sagged as reality set in. What would it matter if he did? So she didn't need the inhaler any more, not even as a talisman.

That didn't change the fact that she was still quiet, sensible Laura, and not the alluring, impulsive woman she'd been pretending to be all weekend, the one whom Adam had been attracted to.

What was it Adam had said? *That's the trouble with adventures. They have to come to an end.* And Laura feared he was right. The best thing she could do was find some courier, express these deeds back to Adam.

And then... Then, she thought with a weary sigh, it was time for Laura Stuart, lady children's author, to go home.

Eleven

The rain drummed against latticed glass doors, which led out onto the patio of Laura's high-rise apartment. She watched it pour down, huddled in the familiar comfort of her fuzzy pink bathrobe and bunny slippers that bore a marked resemblance to her character, Fur Toes. It was past one and she still hadn't troubled to dress. Perhaps she was taking a lesson from the decadent Mr. Storm.

And perhaps she simply wasn't able to rouse enthusiasm for much of anything since returning to Bennington Falls. The dreariness of the day didn't help. By contrast, it only made the whole sunlit weekend seem that much more of a dream, a fantasy like one of those romantic misadventures you watched on late-night TV. But then why did images of Adam keep flashing through her mind, which were all too real, memories of his mouth moving over hers with a reckless heat, of the passion that had flooded between them as wild and relentless as the incoming tide? Or quieter memories of standing with him on the porch of the old Victorian house and sharing a dream, of looking into the deep gray silence of his eyes and somehow knowing, despite the fact she'd been with him for such a short time, that she loved him, would always love him.

No. Laura shoved aside the thought, which only brought an ache to her heart. She returned to her drawing table, trying to resume work on the sketch she'd been working on. But her creation seemed to stare back at her, looking as forlorn as she felt. Fur Toes sat hunched on a tuft of grass, his furry little face pressed against his paws, his ears drooping to his knees.

"What's the matter with you?" Laura chided softly. "Don't you know it was an adventure? Only an adventure."

She started to tear off the sheet of paper, planning to wad it up and send it to join the pile already littering the floor. But she was stopped by the sound of a buzzer, alerting her that someone was in the lobby below, seeking admittance up to her apartment.

She wasn't expecting anyone. Most likely it was some kid selling candy bars or magazines to raise money for his camp or church group. Laura was a noted easy mark in the neighborhood. She went over to flick the switch on her wall intercom.

"Yes?" she said. "Who is it?"

"Hi, kiddo. It's me." Chelsey's voice crackled through the speaker.

Chelsey! Laura hadn't seen her sister since she'd tossed her into the Barnharts' pool. Chelsey rarely ever returned to Bennington Falls these days. Whether she'd come to vent her indignation at Laura or to offer her own brand of brash apologies for the weekend's disaster, Laura wasn't sure she felt up to listening.

"Laura? Laura, are you there?" Chelsey called.

Laura wondered if she could disguise her voice to sound like the cleaning lady, the custodian or even a burglar.

"I know you're there, Laura," Chelsey insisted. "If you don't push the button and let me come up, I'll ring your neighbor, old Mr. McElhinney. He'll let me into the building just to see if I'm wearing a bra, and I'm not sure his pacemaker is up to it."

Chelsey's voice dropped to a more wheedling note. "C'mon, Laura. I'm sorry about getting you involved in all my craziness this weekend. I just want to make things up to you. I brought you a present."

Not immune to that pleading tone, in spite of everything that had happened, Laura relented.

"All right, all right," she said with a soft groan of resignation. She punched the automatic release button that unlocked the main door and waited. A few minutes later, a brisk rap sounded on her apartment door.

Laura took off the chain and swung the door open, coming face to face with...

Adam!

Laura's heart gave a wild lurch. For a moment, all she could do was blink and stare, wondering if she were having an hallucination. Adam looked sexy enough to be any woman's fantasy. His ash gold hair was damp from the rain, the shadowed contours of his face, hard and lean, his chin creased with that dangerous-looking scar. His broad shoulders were encased in a tan raincoat, which could have passed for a trench coat. The spy who came in from the rain shower. Mr. Bond returning from another narrow escape.

But the steady light of his gray eyes, the dripping umbrella he carried in very practical Adam fashion—those details Laura knew she couldn't have imagined. Those were too endearingly real.

"Adam," she quavered when she found her voice. Her pleasure at seeing him was so intense, it was almost painful. Then pleasure dissolved into horror.

She clutched at the front of her woolly pink bathrobe, her other hand flying to her disheveled hair. Doing a quick shuffle step in an effort to hide the bunny slippers, she felt her cheeks fire red hot.

Her first panicky impulse was to dive back into the shelter of her apartment and slam the door. But Adam's arm shot out, preventing her.

"Laura, wait," he said. "I'm sorry for the subterfuge. But after what happened at the beach house, I was afraid if you knew it was me, you wouldn't let me come up."

"What—what are you doing here?" she stammered, still struggling to block the door. "And where's Chelsey?"

Adam managed to insinuate one foot in the door. "I think after that little dunk in the pool you gave her the other day, she's learned to be more cautious. She thought it was more prudent to go run an errand."

"She's right," Laura muttered. "I'm going to kill her for this."

"It wasn't her fault. I had her bring me here. I needed to see you . . . please."

Needed to see her for what? Laura peered warily at him through the gap in the door. She looked for some trace of the anger, the distance she'd last seen in his eyes. There was none, only an expression she found unreadable.

Laura wrestled with her uncertainty a moment more, then surrendered. What did it matter, anyway? Adam already knew she wasn't the sultry femme fatale she had pretended to be. He might as well come in and get his first good look at the real Laura Stuart.

She backed away, letting the door swing open. Adam stepped inside and closed it behind him. He propped his dripping umbrella against the old-fashioned coat stand in the entryway, then turned to face Laura. His eyes skimmed over her. Laura toyed with the belt of her robe, feeling strangely more exposed than when she'd been naked in front of him. Her rabbits seemed to wink up at him, their whiskers twitching into idiotic grins.

Adam stared at the slippers. Laura thought she saw him suppress a tiny smile, but all he said was, "You did a pretty fast disappearing act on Sunday, Miss Stuart. You didn't even leave a forwarding address."

Laura drew herself up with dignity, at least as much dignity as a woman wearing bunny slippers could muster. "I didn't think anyone would be bothering to look me up."

"But I had something to say to you, and I thought it was best said in person."

Laura's pulse skipped a beat. Hope danced through her, foolish, ridiculous, but undeniable hope.

"I needed to thank you for getting those papers back from Storm for me."

"Oh. *That.*" Hope tripped and fell flat on its face. Laura gave a brittle shrug. "That was nothing. You didn't need to drive over two hundred miles to thank me for that."

"Maybe I also felt the need to apologize. I guess I came down pretty hard on you for that switch you and Chelsey pulled."

"And I guess I deserved it."

An awkward silence fell. Laura added wistfully, "And so that's all you wanted to tell me?"

Adam had thought it was. At least, that's what he'd convinced himself on the way up here. He was the kind of man who liked to tie up loose ends, and Laura had vanished from his life a bit too abruptly. And maybe he'd had the tiniest bit of curiosity to see her when she wasn't pretending to be Chelsey.

That was probably why he was having difficulty keeping his eyes off of her. That oversize bathrobe only seemed to emphasize the delicate, creamy texture of her throat, tantalizing him with the lovely curves he knew were hidden beneath those fluffy pink folds. The robe suited her somehow. So did those ridiculous slippers. Better than some of the oversexed clothes she'd been wearing that weekend.

Laura's hair tumbled about her shoulders, soft and brown, golden like the morning sun. Her eyes seemed huge in her pale face. Never had she looked more gentle, more vulnerable. Never had she looked more alluring.

Adam grimaced. How was it possible to feel this sudden surge of desire for a woman wearing rabbit slippers? To cover the rising confusion of his emotions, he turned away to study her apartment.

It was like a bout of déjà vu. It was all so warm and familiar to him, the wingback chair with the homey afghan draped over, the white lacy doilies adoring fragile mahogany end tables, the old oak rocking chair with its needlework cushions, the row of African violets that bloomed on one windowsill. Somehow he could have guessed she would prefer such surroundings as these. No, not guess. He had known.

Trailing after him, Laura watched Adam's inspection of her apartment, feeling anxious and uncomfortable. His presence here still mystified her. She couldn't believe he'd driven so far just to thank her or to offer that stiff apology.

Maybe like Luke and Chelsey, Adam thought that he and Laura could now be friends. The prospect was depressing enough to make her want to throw herself off the balcony.

When Adam paused by her sketching table, Laura felt her agitation only increase.

"Is this where you work?" he asked.

"Yes."

"Are you starting a new book?"

"Yes, but it's not going very well."

This was ridiculous, Laura thought, grinding her teeth. Now they were chatting about her book. She'd once made love to this man on a windswept beach and now they were acting like casual acquaintances. No, worse than that. They were behaving as awkwardly as teenagers on a first date.

Adam studied her sketch she'd left pinned to the board, Fur Toes in all his misery.

"Your friend there certainly doesn't look very happy," he commented.

Neither was she. Adam was beginning to make her a little crazy. But she sighed and explained. "In this story, Fur Toes's family is moving, you see. And Fur Toes has never adapted well to change."

She winced. She'd always had a habit of talking about her characters as though they were real. Adam would think she was nuts. But to her astonishment, he agreed with her.

"Yes, I can understand why he's so disgruntled. I don't take too well to changes or surprises, either. And it seems to fit with his character. I remember Fur Toes didn't like it when his friend the otter went away, or when the old ice pond had to be shut down."

Laura stared at Adam, her jaw dropping open. Then she gasped, "You—you've been reading my books."

He squirmed beneath her accusing look, appearing a little sheepish.

"I can't believe it," she said. "The man who grew up on *Architectural Digest* has suddenly developed an interest in Fur Toes Rabbit?"

Adam shrugged. "I was curious, that's all. I seem to be curious lately about a lot of things."

"Like what?"

"Like why you decided to go to Atlantic City and take Storm by the throat to get my papers back."

It was Laura's turn to squirm. "It wasn't quite that heroic. Storm would probably have returned the deeds, anyway."

"Still, I have a strange feeling that confronting ruthless tycoons is not Miss L.C. Stuart's usual style. Why'd you do it, Laura?" Adam persisted.

"I—I hated to see that lovely old house destroyed."

"Is that the only reason?"

Laura couldn't meet his eyes.

"I was hoping it might be the same reason I got so upset when I discovered the truth about your identity," he said. "It was hard for me to admit, but I realize now why I was so shaken up."

"And why's that?" Laura whispered, her heart beginning to thud painfully.

Adam gave a shaky laugh. "It's going to sound insane, impossible, but . . . I'm sure I'm in love with you. In fact, I've never been more damn sure of anything in my life."

A glad cry breached Laura's lips. "Oh, Adam, I love you, too."

But as he started toward her, she shrank back, shaking her head, reality checking in again. "No, Adam, this is crazy. You don't really know anything about me."

"I know you can't swim and you're a lousy photographer."

"You know what I'm not. But you don't know what I am. Look around you," Laura said miserably. She waved her hand in a wild, demonstrative arc. "There's nothing glamorous or exciting about me. I spend most of my days within these four walls, watching the world pass by my window. I—I like Victorian blouses and pink bathrobes. And I draw rabbits. I *wear* rabbits."

"I never had anything against rabbits. I think I could even get to like them, except—" He reached inside his coat and drew out a rumpled sheet of paper. "I found this in a drawer after you had gone. I remember what you once said about turning people into rabbits."

He held up her drawing of the stuffy little rabbit with the spectacles slipping down his nose.

"Uncle Cawwots?" he demanded with fierce indignation.

Laura blushed, her lips trembling with a guilty smile. "Every family should have one."

Then suddenly the sketch was fluttering to the floor and she was in Adam's arms. His mouth covered hers in a kiss that was hard and possessive, then softened to a tenderness that brought tears to her eyes.

She buried her face against his shoulder, his coat smelling of fresh summer rain and Adam's own musky cologne. She murmured, "Are you really certain about this, Adam? Because if you were mistaken, I—I don't think I could bear—"

"I'm certain," he murmured, his face resting warm against her hair. "I love you, Laura. I was wrong that night when I said I didn't know you. I do."

"You said you couldn't tell the difference between me and Chelsey."

"I could pick you out if you had a hundred twin sisters. I spent time with Chelsey on the way up here. She's an interesting girl, but she's not you."

"If she was any more interesting, she'd be the death of me," Laura said in muffled accents against his shoulder.

Adam chuckled. Brushing her hair back gently, he forced Laura to look up. "Did you ever stop to think it wasn't really Chelsey you were pretending to be? These past few days you might've finally been free to be yourself. I know that's what happened to me."

"But who is it you think I am, Adam?"

Adam gazed down at her tenderly and whispered a kiss across her lips. "A warm, compassionate woman. One who'd take any crazy risk for the people you care about, from trying to pose as a photographer of nudes, to cornering one of the most powerful men in Atlantic City."

Warm, compassionate. How nice, Laura thought glumly.

"But—but I want to be . . . seductive," she protested.

Adam kissed the tip of her nose. "You can seduce a man with those great green eyes of yours, right down to his soul."

"My eyes?" Laura asked wistfully. "Is that the only thing you admire? I know I don't have much up top, but my legs aren't so bad."

"I know all about your legs. And I never found fault with what's up top, either." His voice dropped to a throaty growl, and his next kiss was not so light and playful.

His mouth moved over hers, warm, demanding, coaxing her lips apart. His tongue dueled with hers in a way that was hot, intimate, setting up a rhythm that Laura could feel pulsing through her blood. Desire simmered between them as it had since they'd first met, like a crackling of electricity.

Adam clasped her hard against him, leaving her in no doubt of his wants, needs. Her own body throbbed with a mutual longing, but still she felt a part of her holding back, afraid.

"Oh, Adam," she faltered. "What—what if it's not the same . . . Making love to me as Laura in a bed. No moonlight, no sea breezes, no beach. What if the magic isn't there?"

"Well, there's only one way to find out, isn't there?"

His eyes met hers, dark, hazy, the look alone enough to make Laura feel as if she were on fire.

She shivered, nodded. Adam scooped her up in his arms. Finding her bedroom, he carried her inside, setting her on her feet beside her big brass bed.

She helped him shrug out of his raincoat, eager to demonstrate that he wasn't the only one who was good with buttons. But as Adam started to kiss her again, she experienced another attack of shyness, uncertainty.

"Adam," she murmured, holding him off. "I know you don't like surprises, changes. But there has been one change, even since you've known me."

"And what's that?" he asked tenderly.

Laura swallowed, but there was no way she could explain something so. . . embarrassingly intimate. There was nothing she could do except show him. With unsteady fingers, she undid the belt of her robe and let it slowly pool to the floor.

She was wearing nothing underneath except for a wisp of black lace panties.

Adam sucked in his breath, and a visible shudder coursed through him. Something flared in his eyes, and his hands became clumsy with the effort to tear free of his own clothes.

They stretched out side by side on her bed, naked. Laura pressed close to him, feeling her eagerness mount, to touch, to taste, to feel him moving inside her, to try to recapture those glorious moments they'd known on the beach.

But this time it was Adam who hesitated, a peculiar look crossing his face.

"Uh, Laura, I'm sure I'll get used to those rabbits of yours eventually. But right now, they're staring at me."

Caught up in the flood of passion, it took Laura a moment to figure out what he was talking about. Then she realized. She was still wearing her bunny slippers. Laughing, she kicked them off her feet.

Then her laughter stilled as Adam drew her close, molding her body perfectly to the hard, pulsing length of his. As his mouth met hers, all hesitations dissolved.

They kissed, caressed, the fever mounting, the familiar magic pulsing between them. They became two people lost to all sense of time, of place, aware of nothing but each other, the wonder of the feelings they shared.

Long moments later, when she lay spent in Adam's arms, Laura knew all her doubts had been stilled. Forever.

She nestled against the warmth of his bare shoulder, the contented silence wrapping around them, as deep and intimate as their lovemaking had been.

Adam stirred at last, brushing a kiss against her brow. "So what do you think, Miss Stuart?" he asked. "Do you think you could ever be happy living in an old Victorian house, raising half a dozen kids by the sea?"

Was he serious? Laura shot up, propping onto one elbow to stare down at him. "Is this a proposal of marriage, Mr. Barnhart? After one weekend?"

"Actually, Lou will wonder what took me so long. She claims she could tell you were right for me as soon as you came through the door."

"It's all that golfing. It must do wonders for her eyesight. But seriously, Adam, neither of us is that impulsive. Maybe we should take things a bit more slowly."

"Seriously, Laura," he murmured, caressing her cheek. "I'm as scared as you are by how hard and fast this has all come upon us. But we'll work it out. Just give me a chance to get to know you better."

"How much time do you want, Mr. Barnhart?"

"Not much. Only the rest of your life." Drawing her close, he kissed her. "With the blood tests and the license and everything, I figure we can be married by the end of the week."

Laura smiled mistily. That's what she loved about the man. He was so sane, so sensible, just like she was.

Easing back into his arms, she gave him her answer with her kiss.

* * * * *

It's our 1000th
Silhouette Romance
and we're celebrating!

Join us for a special collection of love stories by the authors you've loved for years, and new favorites you've just discovered.

It's a celebration just for you,
with wonderful books by
Diana Palmer, Suzanne Carey,
Tracy Sinclair, Marie Ferrarella,
Debbie Macomber, Laurie Paige,
Annette Broadrick, Elizabeth August
and MORE!

Silhouette Romance...vibrant, fun and emotionally rich! Take another look at us!

As part of the celebration, readers can receive a FREE gift AND enter our exciting sweepstakes to win a grand prize of $1000! Look for more details in all March Silhouette series titles.

You'll fall in love all over again
with Silhouette Romance!

Silhouette® ™

CEL1000T

Relive the romance...
Harlequin and Silhouette
are proud to present

by Request™

A program of collections of three complete novels by the most requested authors with the most requested themes. Be sure to look for one volume each month with three complete novels by top name authors.

In January: **WESTERN LOVING** — Susan Fox, JoAnn Ross, Barbara Kaye

Loving a cowboy is easy—taming him isn't!

In February: **LOVER, COME BACK!** — Diana Palmer, Lisa Jackson, Patricia Gardner Evans

It was over so long ago—yet now they're calling, "Lover, Come Back!"

In March: **TEMPERATURE RISING** — JoAnn Ross, Tess Gerritsen, Jacqueline Diamond

Falling in love—just what the doctor ordered!

Available at your favorite retail outlet.

REQ-G3

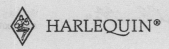

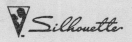

HARLEQUIN®   Silhouette

SILHOUETTE®

Desire®

SAXON BROTHERS

An exciting new trilogy from JACKIE MERRITT

Chance, Rush and Cash—three sinfully sexy brothers who would turn any woman's head! Don't miss:

March **WRANGLER'S LADY**—Chance is one handsome Montana rancher, and this *Man of the Month* knows what he wants—and how to get her!

April **MYSTERY LADY**—The desert heat of Nevada is nothing compared to the sparks that sexy Rush ignites in one mysterious woman!

May **PERSISTENT LADY**—The untamed wilderness of Oregon and one persistent female are no match for determined bachelor Cash!

Let the SAXON BROTHERS keep you warm at night—only from Silhouette Desire!

SDSAX1

SILHOUETTE... Where Passion Lives

Don't miss these Silhouette favorites by some of our most distinguished authors! And now you can receive a discount by ordering two or more titles!

SD	#05772	FOUND FATHER by Justine Davis	$2.89	☐
SD	#05783	DEVIL OR ANGEL by Audra Adams	$2.89	☐
SD	#05786	QUICKSAND by Jennifer Greene	$2.89	☐
SD	#05796	CAMERON by Beverly Barton	$2.99	☐
IM	#07481	FIREBRAND by Paula Detmer Riggs	$3.39	☐
IM	#07502	CLOUD MAN by Barbara Faith	$3.50	☐
IM	#07505	HELL ON WHEELS by Naomi Horton	$3.50	☐
IM	#07512	SWEET ANNIE'S PASS by Marilyn Pappano	$3.50	☐
SE	#09791	THE CAT THAT LIVED ON PARK AVENUE by Tracy Sinclair	$3.39	☐
SE	#09793	FULL OF GRACE by Ginna Ferris	$3.39	☐
SE	#09822	WHEN SOMEBODY WANTS by Trisha Alexander	$3.50	☐
SE	#09841	ON HER OWN by Pat Warren	$3.50	☐
SR	#08866	PALACE CITY PRINCE by Arlene James	$2.69	☐
SR	#08916	UNCLE DADDY by Kasey Michaels	$2.69	☐
SR	#08948	MORE THAN YOU KNOW by Phyllis Halldorson	$2.75	☐
SR	#08954	HERO IN DISGUISE by Stella Bagwell	$2.75	☐
SS	#27006	NIGHT MIST by Helen R. Myers	$3.50	☐
SS	#27010	IMMINENT THUNDER by Rachel Lee	$3.50	☐
SS	#27015	FOOTSTEPS IN THE NIGHT by Lee Karr	$3.50	☐
SS	#27020	DREAM A DEADLY DREAM by Allie Harrison	$3.50	☐

(limited quantities available on certain titles)

AMOUNT $

DEDUCT: **10% DISCOUNT FOR 2+ BOOKS** $

POSTAGE & HANDLING $________

($1.00 for one book, 50¢ for each additional)

APPLICABLE TAXES* $________

TOTAL PAYABLE $________

(check or money order—please do not send cash)

To order, complete this form and send it, along with a check or money order for the total above, payable to Silhouette Books, to: **In the U.S.:** 3010 Walden Avenue, P.O. Box 9077, Buffalo, NY 14269-9077; **In Canada:** P.O. Box 636, Fort Erie, Ontario, L2A 5X3.

Name: ________________

Address: ____________ City: ____________

State/Prov.: ____________ Zip/Postal Code: ____________

*New York residents remit applicable sales taxes.
Canadian residents remit applicable GST and provincial taxes. SBACK-JM

Silhouette® TM

SILHOUETTE®
Desire®

JOAN JOHNSTON'S

HAWK'S WAY

SERIES CONTINUES!

Available in March, *The Cowboy Takes a Wife* (D #842) is the latest addition to Joan Johnston's sexy series about the lives and loves of the irresistible Whitelaw family. Set on a Wyoming ranch, this heart-wrenching story tells the tale of a single mother who desperately needs a husband—a very *big* husband—fast!

Don't miss *The Cowboy Takes a Wife* by Joan Johnston, only from Silhouette Desire.

To order earlier titles by Joan Johnston about the Whitelaw family, *Honey and the Hired Hand* (D #746, 11/92), *The Cowboy and the Princess* (D #785, 5/93) or *The Wrangler and the Rich Girl* (D #791, 6/93) send your name, address, zip or postal code, along with a check or money order (please do not send cash) for $2.89 for D #746 and #785 and $2.99 for D #791, plus 75¢ postage and handling ($1.00 in Canada), payable to Silhouette Books, to:

In the U.S.
Silhouette Books
3010 Walden Ave.
P. O. Box 9077
Buffalo, NY 14269-9077

In Canada
Silhouette Books
P. O. Box 636
Fort Erie, Ontario
L2A 5X3

Please specify book title(s) with order.
Canadian residents add applicable federal and provincial taxes. SDHW4

SPRING Fancy '94

They're sexy, single...
and about to get snagged!

Passion is in full bloom as love catches the fancy of three brash bachelors. You won't want to miss these stories by three of Silhouette's hottest authors:

CAIT LONDON
DIXIE BROWNING
PEPPER ADAMS

Spring fever is in the air this March—
and there's no avoiding it!

Only from

Silhouette® TM

where passion lives.

SF94

MEN MADE IN AMERICA

Fifty red-blooded, white-hot, true-blue hunks from every State in the Union!

Look for MEN MADE IN AMERICA! Written by some of our most poplar authors, these stories feature fifty of the strongest, sexiest men, each from a different state in the union!

Two titles available every other month at your favorite retail outlet.

In January, look for:

DREAM COME TRUE by Ann Major (Florida)
WAY OF THE WILLOW by Linda Shaw (Georgia)

In March, look for:

TANGLED LIES by Anne Stuart (Hawaii)
ROGUE'S VALLEY by Kathleen Creighton (Idaho)

You won't be able to resist MEN MADE IN AMERICA!

If you missed your state or would like to order any other states that have already been published, send your name, address, zip or postal code along with a check or money order (please do not send cash) for $3.59 for each book, plus 75¢ postage and handling ($1.00 in Canada), payable to Harlequin Reader Service, to:

In the U.S.
3010 Walden Avenue
P.O. Box 1369
Buffalo, NY 14269-1369

In Canada
P.O. Box 609
Fort Erie, Ontario
L2A 5X3

Please specify book title(s) with your order.
Canadian residents add applicable federal and provincial taxes.

MEN194